UNDER CLOCK AND KEY

The Thief's Apprentice ~ Book Three

SARA C ROETHLE

Vulture's Eye Publications

❀ Created with Vellum

CHAPTER 1

Arhyen slammed his fist against the white-painted metal door. "You can't keep me in here forever!" he yelled, despite knowing his efforts were futile. He should never have allowed Liliana to talk him into this. Accepting aid from the London Network, the very organization he'd sworn to bring down, was just asking for trouble. That Hamlet had arranged the whole set up was only the icing on an exceedingly bitter cake.

He paced around the sterile room, scowling at the white mattress on top of a wheeled cart that served as his bed. The London Network had tended his surgery wounds, ensuring his body would not reject the new synthetic organs placed within him, sure, but it was all for naught if they wouldn't let him *leave*.

It had been two weeks since he'd last seen Liliana or Ephraim. Hamlet had escorted him to the facility, though he barely remembered the journey. He'd let the apparent infection in his wounds go for too long, and had only blearily agreed to being looked at by the LN's surgeons, lest he succumb to his maladies. A few days into his treatment, he regained awareness. At first, he'd been too weak and ill to enquire about his eventual release, but after the first five days, once he'd felt well enough to think straight, he'd begun to worry. He'd received no word from Hamlet, Liliana, or *anyone*.

He knew Liliana would not leave him trapped there by choice . . . would she? She'd been furious with him for refusing to seek help until he was too ill to decline, but he *had* finally agreed. Tears filled her eyes when Hamlet led him away to the sterile, underground surgery. Tears that said I'll miss you and I'll be here once you're better. So where was she?

He stroked his stubbly chin as he glared at the door one last time, then stalked across the room, swatting angrily at the white surgical gown he'd been forced to wear, leaving his legs vulnerable to cold drafts, not to mention the hit his pride took anytime someone observed him in the garment . . . and there'd been *plenty* of someones, all looking him over with the uncaring eyes of surgeons and scientists, as if he were little more than an experiment gone wrong.

He plopped down on his *bed*, glancing at the stack of books he'd been given to occupy his time, but he'd already read them all. It didn't matter, he was sure another surgeon, or alchemist, or lowly orderly would be along soon to poke and prod him. He'd lost count of how many vials of blood were taken, how many lights shined into his eyes, how many times he'd been asked to attempt superhuman feats . . .

The latter still eluded him.

Hazel, his long lost sister, now deceased, had kidnapped him with the intent of turning him into something like her, something similar to an automaton, but with human origins. He wasn't sure of all that had been done to him, and any evidence had been burned along with the old farmhouse where he'd been held, but he knew he'd been given new organs, and perhaps his brain had been altered, though he wasn't sure. He didn't currently feel like a single-focused psychopath, and that's what his sister had turned into after her own alterations. If it was just his organs, perhaps he'd simply function a little more efficiently now that the infection was under control.

Liliana could heal remarkably fast, run for ages without tiring, and leap over fences like a cat. Perhaps he'd get *those* skills, and they could all move on with their lives . . . if he was ever let out of this bloody room.

He couldn't help but think that perhaps *Codename Hamlet*, or just Hamlet for short, was keeping Liliana away. He'd manipulated her in the past by pretending to be something other than a ruthless killing machine. Was he with her now, having a cup of tea and telling her Arhyen would be just fine without her?

He lifted one of the nearby books and hurled it across the room, glaring at it as it thudded against the wall then fell to the concrete floor. He needed to get out of this cursed room before it was too late. Hamlet had to be stopped at all costs.

He rose to his feet and strode across the room to resume his pounding on the door. If he couldn't escape on his own, he'd simply use his powers of annoyance until someone became fed up enough to let him go.

❧

LILIANA TOOK A SHAKY BREATH, THEN LOWERED HER face back to the microscope, though she knew it would reveal nothing new. The scrap of paper she observed contained a vibrant blue stain, just a small sample of the liquid covering nearly every surface in the previous dwelling of the Captain of the Watch. The same Captain who had confessed to murder and conspiracy to conceal evidence roughly two weeks prior.

His confession had cleared Ephraim Godwin, one of the few men in London Liliana could trust, of his alleged crimes. Once he'd been reinstated, Ephraim's first order of business was investigating the extent of the previous Captain's crimes, while the Captain himself awaited trial. Ephraim had found little to arouse suspicion, except the presence of the vibrant blue liquid.

Upon first glance, Liliana had deemed it simple ink, but that arose the question, where had all the ink come from? There had been some broken glass amongst the puddles of vibrant blue, but so shattered, they'd been rendered unidentifiable. Ephraim had insisted on testing the liquid, but no longer trusted any members of the Watch, as it likely took more than just the Captain to frame him for murder. So, it had fallen to Liliana to investigate, a task she was more than willing to take on, if only to distract herself from Arhyen's absence.

Pulling her face away from the view of the now-dry vibrant liquid beneath the microscope lens, she pushed a strand of red hair back into her bun and glanced around Arhyen's silent apartment. She had attempted once to visit him, but Hamlet had prevented her. According to him, the London Network would gladly apprehend her for questioning, and that was something that would only cause further complications for Arhyen. Hamlet would ensure that Arhyen was released once fully recovered.

Fighting away tears, and perhaps a bit of guilt, she turned her thoughts back to the mystery before her. One of the initial tests she'd run on the liquid was the application of phenolphthalein, a weak acid that could be used to determine various properties within any unknown liquid. This particular test had revealed the presence of human cells, not just in a small sampling, but in numerous samplings of the liquid obtained from different areas of the home. So, either someone had mixed a bit of their blood into all the vibrant ink before use, or the liquid was not ink at all, but some unknown biologic compound.

A knock on the door drew her out of her thoughts. Remaining seated on the sofa, she reached across the low table toward Arhyen's pocket watch, flipping open the gold face to reveal it was half past noon, thirty minutes before Ephraim was supposed to arrive.

Slowly, she stood, careful not to make any noise, then crept across the room toward the door. Holding up the skirts of her long sleeved, high-collared, magenta dress, she stepped over the tripwire in the entryway, then onto a small stool to peer through the peephole in the upper portion of the door. Her shoulders slumped as she recognized the woman outside. *Catherine*.

She climbed down from the stool, debating whether to open the door at all. Another encounter with Arhyen's estranged mother was the last thing she needed . . . but on the other hand, Catherine had been somewhat involved in Arhyen's kidnapping and subsequent surgeries. Perhaps she came bearing useful information. Information that would mean Liliana should race across town to Arhyen and *demand* to see him, if only to deliver the invaluable news.

Shaking her head at her runaway thoughts, she stepped down from the stool, pushed it aside, then unlatched the numerous locks lining the door. She left the security chain in place, opening the door just enough to reveal her face and a sliver of her body.

Catherine waited outside patiently, dressed all in mourner's black. Liliana could only assume her garb was out of respect for Hazel, her recently departed daughter. Her recently departed, part-automaton, *psychopath* daughter.

"What do you want?" Liliana demanded, feeling little pity for the woman after the way she'd treated Arhyen.

The lines on Catherine's face deepened into a frown. Liliana hated that she could see a bit of Arhyen in her expression and in her trim build.

"Honestly," she began, "I was hoping to ask your automaton *friend* for a favor, one I think he owes me after leaving me locked in that cellar for two days."

Liliana raised her hand to her mouth, too late to disguise her gasp. *Two days?* She knew Hamlet had stored Catherine somewhere safe before they'd moved on to the farmhouse to find Arhyen, but she hadn't been aware he'd neglected to release her in a timely manner, though she supposed it was likely a result of Hamlet's grave injuries. He'd been in no shape to re-enter the city right away.

Shoving her sympathy to the back of her mind, Liliana narrowed her eyes. "You know, it is not wise to ask favors of someone who'd sooner kill you than help you."

Catherine's frown deepened. "I see *you're* becoming more human every day, just as bitter as the rest of us."

That gave Liliana pause. Was she more bitter now? The past two weeks had been difficult for her, worrying about Arhyen while attempting to help Ephraim with his mystery. Perhaps she'd sunk to wallowing in bitterness and self-pity once or twice.

She sighed, then forced a small smile on her face. "What is the favor you'd like to ask?"

Catherine's gaze shifted nervously. "May I come in? I'd rather not speak out in the open."

Liliana glanced over her shoulder at the rest of the apartment, currently hidden from Catherine's view. Her research was strewn all about, along with a few small explosives she'd been working on, but she supposed Catherine wouldn't know what any of it was. She'd likely just think her a slob, obsessed with vibrant blue ink and tiny glass vials.

She turned her gaze forward to look Catherine up and down. If worse came to worst, she could at least best Catherine in a physical confrontation, so there should be little to worry about. Nodding, she shut the door to slide the security chain out of its track, then reopened it to admit Catherine, who hurried in without a second glance.

Liliana grabbed her arm before she could activate the tripwire in the threshold, pulling her backward just before her boot could spring the trap.

"Careful where you walk," Liliana advised, releasing Catherine's arm to shut the door behind them.

Catherine stood perfectly still until Liliana stepped around her, over the tripwire, then led the way to the sofa. She'd disarmed many of the traps Arhyen had placed around the apartment before his incident, but had felt oddly guilty about disarming them *all*, so a few still remained.

Reaching the sofa, she gestured for Catherine to sit.

Glancing around warily, Catherine lowered her bony frame to the blue, threadbare cushions. She cast her eye across the scattered papers and microscope on the low table.

Resisting the urge to sweep everything out of sight,

Liliana smoothed her skirts and stepped around the table to take a seat next to Catherine. "Now what is this favor?"

"Well," Catherine began, "as you know, working for Hazel," her voice cracked at the mention of her deceased daughter, "I was afforded a measure of protection," she continued bravely. "The moment I told you and your automaton about the farmhouse, I lost *everything*. Not just my daughter, but my home, my livelihood, *everything*."

Liliana pursed her lips before she could say something venomous. "You act as if you made a choice to help us for the greater good when you were merely attempting to save your own skin."

"Be that as it may," Catherine continued patiently, "you and your *associate* took my life from me. Now, I have nothing."

Liliana sighed, warring with the sympathy threatening to surface. "What do you want?" she muttered.

Catherine's lip twitched into a brief smirk, quickly disguised with a hopeful smile. "I would like to become connected to the notorious London Network. The *real* London Network, not the various splinter groups."

Liliana narrowed her gaze. *Various* splinter groups? She knew Hazel's group had branched away from the *LN*, and was somehow associated with Viola Walmsley, at least according to Hamlet. Of course, Viola and Hazel were both dead now, so there was no way of knowing for sure. How many others could still be out there?

"Why would you want that?" she asked finally.

Catherine rolled her eyes. "Of course *you* would ask that. You have my son to take care of you, and that *detective*. I have no one. London is not kind to unmarried women of my age, especially ones without estates or meaningless titles. I've survived thus far by making myself useful to organizations capable of providing me with coin and protection. You have left me with nothing."

A knock sounded at the door.

Seeming suddenly nervous, Catherine flicked her eyes toward the sound. "My son?" she whispered.

Liliana searched Catherine's face for any hint of deception. Did she truly not know Arhyen hadn't been home for two weeks? Perhaps she really was on her own now, without any spies or henchmen to do her bidding. Perhaps she always had been.

"It's Ephraim," she explained, rising from the sofa.

Catherine scowled as she stood. "Then that is my cue to depart. Please think upon my request." She withdrew a small piece of parchment from her coat pocket and offered it to Liliana. "You can find me at this address, for now. Though I imagine I'll need to move soon." Not waiting for a reply, she breezed past Liliana toward the door, hesitating for a split-second before stepping over the tripwire and letting herself outside.

Standing near the doorway, Ephraim watched her go silently, then quirked a questioning blond brow at Liliana.

She gestured tiredly for him to come in.

He removed his black fedora as he entered, then shut the door behind him. He'd stepped over the tripwire enough times that he didn't hesitate, and instead strolled confidently across the room to remove his black coat, placing it on the back of the sofa along with his fedora.

Not bothering to ask permission, he circled the sofa then plopped down on a cushion, leaning forward to peer through Liliana's microscope.

She moved toward the stove to make tea, keeping in line with their usual noontime ritual, established shortly after Arhyen agreed to allow the LN's surgeons to care for him.

"Do you actually gain anything from observing objects so closely?" Ephraim questioned, still peering through the lens.

Liliana set the filled teapot on the stove, then glanced over her shoulder at his hunched back. "You gain *everything* from looking at objects so closely," she explained. "The human eye is comparatively weak, prone to missing evidence of the utmost importance."

Ephraim snorted, then leaned back against the sofa cushions to eye her speculatively. "One of these days I'm going to read all of your detective novels, then your numerous observations won't seem quite so smart."

She rolled her eyes at him, then turned back to the kettle, waiting for it to whistle. Perhaps she'd quoted from one of her novels word for word, but he'd never know for sure if he never found that particular book. What she'd said had been true regardless, though the microscope hadn't helped her in this case.

Once the water was ready she finished preparing the tea, then placed two cups on a small tray and carried it over to the low table in front of the sofa.

"Any word from Arhyen?" Ephraim inquired, lifting his tea for a sip.

Liliana frowned, then walked around the table to sit on the other end of the sofa. "I think I should go down there," she admitted. "Hamlet cautioned that I should not draw attention to myself, but I feel I can stay away no longer. It's been two weeks. Surely he should have been released by now?"

Ephraim nodded. "I'm still not sure at what point we began trusting Hamlet to begin with. If Arhyen hadn't been knocking at death's door, I would have voted we stay as far away from Hamlet as possible."

A feeling of unease clenched Liliana's gut. At one point, she would have agreed that trusting Hamlet was unwise. Perhaps she still did. After all, she hadn't heard from him in a week. "He helped me save Arhyen's life. I don't see why he would do all that he's done, simply to turn around and hold him hostage."

"Perhaps he's not the one doing the holding?" Ephraim suggested.

She took a sip of her cooling tea. "You mean the LN? Perhaps they want Arhyen for other reasons that have nothing to do with Hamlet?"

Ephraim nodded. "He has information they would like to keep secret. Few know of the synthetic emotions created by your father and Victor Ashdown."

She pursed her lips and set her tea on the table. "*We* know, yet we're still here."

"So something else then," he continued. "Perhaps they want to further observe his new . . . parts."

"So they could be experimenting on him?" she gasped. Sure, she'd considered it, but she'd been under the impression Hamlet would stop that from happening . . . but Hamlet wasn't around. He could be dead for all she knew.

Ephraim shrugged and took another sip of his tea.

Liliana resisted the urge to punch him for being so calm. "What do we do?" she asked instead.

He shrugged again. "We rescue him, I suppose. We can't just wait around for Hamlet to show up again."

She stood, then started searching around the room for any supplies she might need for the mission. "I'll just grab a few things," she muttered, "then we'll go."

Still seated on the sofa, Ephraim cleared his throat.

She paused her search long enough to turn a questioning gaze to him.

He sighed, "You do realize it's only noon? Perhaps we should wait until this evening."

"Ah," she replied, suddenly feeling silly. She quickly resumed her seat beside him, barely able to contain her nervous energy.

"Now tell me what you've uncovered about our mysterious liquid," he instructed, gesturing to the blue-stained papers and items scattered across the low table. "If this is what made a dying man confess to his crimes and give up on his quest to cure his terminal illness, I'd like to know just what this substance is, and if it could be a danger to others."

Liliana shrugged, not overly interested in the blue liquid. "Perhaps the Captain confessed to clear his conscience before he died."

Ephraim snorted. "My dear, in a city like this, men of power have no conscience."

She frowned, her eyes scanning the blue-stained evidence. "In that case, I'm glad neither you nor Arhyen are men of power."

Seeming to take no offense, Ephraim chuckled, then slowly sipped his tea. "No, my dear," he mused, "we most surely are *not*."

❧

ARHYEN'S GAZE TRACED THE WATER STAINS ON THE ceiling above him. He shifted on his makeshift bed uncomfortably. His hands were sore from pounding on the door, as was his mind. Would he simply have to wait for someone to rescue him *again*? It had been humiliating enough to need rescue from his own deranged sister, but now, just weeks later, he found himself in a similar predicament. At least he wasn't being operated on this time . . . yet. He had no illusions on the London Network's capabilities to execute unspeakable horrors.

He sat up with a jolt as the metal door to his small room swung inward. In walked a man with neatly trimmed gray hair and a heavy gray moustache. His lightly lined face was void of expression, just as prim and proper as his uniform, which Arhyen recognized as belonging to the Queen's Guard.

What on earth was a member of the Queen's Guard doing in a LN facility? Unless, he was an imposter, but then that begged the question, why would a member of the LN be posing as a member of the Queen's Guard?

The man eyed Arhyen cooly as he strode into the room, followed by two men in unremarkable black clothing and heavy military boots. The door swung shut behind them.

Arhyen jumped up from his bed, covering as much of himself as possible in the surgical gown.

"Mr. Croft," announced the gray-haired man, clearly the leader of the group. "My name is Sir Thaddeus Wakefield, Captain of the Queen's Guard."

Arhyen's eyes narrowed. Clearly an imposter, then. There was no way the *Captain* of the Queen's Guard would step down from his high horse to talk to a lowly thief in a surgical gown.

The alleged Thaddeus Wakefield turned his cool gaze to one of the black-clad men who hopped to attention, hustling across the small room to retrieve a chair for the *Captain*.

Offering no further acknowledgment to the man who retrieved the small wooden chair, Wakefield sat, then gestured for Arhyen to do the same, though the only place he had to sit was his bed.

Arhyen shook his head defiantly, clasping his hands behind his back. He was no child and would not be lectured as if he were. It felt nice being strong enough now to keep his footing, and to not have his infected incisions stretching uncomfortably with the smallest movements, but those positives were distant thoughts.

"Who are you really, and what do you want?" he demanded.

Wakefield glowered. "I've already told you who I am, and I want information on *Codename Hamlet*. It was he who arranged for you to be brought here, was it not?"

Arhyen glowered right back at him. "Yes, but only under pain of death. And why would you need information on your own operative?" he added, unable to restrain his curiosity.

"He's missing," Wakefield admitted. "As you seem to have become quite . . . interactive with him, you know the dangers he might pose."

Arhyen snorted, then finally lowered himself to the bed before his feet betrayed him. "And why should I care about the London Network's problems?"

Wakefield smiled bitterly. "Well, it would seem you are now indebted to us. Our operative reclaimed you from our fugitive members, and even brought you here for care."

"The same operative you cannot find," Arhyen stated bluntly.

Wakefield inclined his head. "Indeed. The same operative that must be found, before we will consider your release."

Arhyen's jaw dropped. So that's why they were keeping him? They hoped he could somehow instigate

Hamlet's return? "Well I can't very well find him if I'm locked in here," he persuaded. "If you want my help, you'll have to let me go."

Wakefield sneered. "No, I think not. Codename Hamlet has grown . . . unruly. He has been disobeying orders, slaughtering innocent people. Yet *you* are somehow important to him. He requested we save you when you should have been disposed of along with the other evidence. We believe he is protecting others, involving himself in things he does not understand. All we need from you are names. If these names lead us to Hamlet, you shall be released."

Arhyen wiped the sickly sweat from his brow. He knew it had been a bad idea to come here, even if it was the only reason he was currently alive. "Why should I trust a single thing you say? If I give you the names, then you'll no longer have a reason to keep me alive."

Wakefield's moustache bristled as he stood, clearly offended. "Mr. Croft, I am the Captain of the Queen's Guard. I am a man of my word."

Arhyen rolled his eyes. "And why would the Captain of the Queen's Guard be working for the London Network?"

Wakefield scoffed. "My boy, it is called the *London* Network. Who do you believe runs this entire operation?"

Arhyen let out an abrupt laugh at the absurd notion, then the idea slowly sunk in. The London Network had been somehow managing not to draw the attention of the Watch nor the Guard for years. They seemed to have unlimited power and information. They allegedly owned buildings all over the city, yet no one seemed to know how these facilities were obtained, nor how they avoided notice. One of the few people that might have enough power to run such a massive operation was . . . the Queen. *Ye gods.*

"I see you now understand the gravity of this situation," Wakefield observed, lacing his arms behind his back. His minions stood behind him silently, obviously unsurprised by the news that had caused Arhyen such a shock. "I will let you think upon this," Wakefield continued. "Let one of my associates know when you are ready to talk."

With that, he turned on his heel and marched out of the room, followed by his men in black.

Arhyen watched on in stunned silence as the door shut behind them. The London Network was run by . . . the Queen? He had to tell Ephraim and Liliana. They had gotten themselves into a mess they couldn't possibly comprehend. He had to—he stared at the sealed door—he had to do bloody *nothing*. He was stuck in this tiny room, and there was no way he'd be giving them Ephraim and Liliana's names *now*. He still couldn't even believe that Hamlet had somehow protected their identities in the first place. What was it all for?

He slumped back onto his bed and stared once again at the water-stained ceiling. His best hope was to trust that Hamlet had some sort of plan in bringing him there, and that really wasn't a hope at all. If his life depended on Hamlet's reappearance, he was easily as good as dead.

CHAPTER 2

Liliana's warm breath fogged the cool night air. She wore what she thought of as her *stealthy ensemble*, made up of black women's equestrian trousers, a blouse, and soft soled boots. Her hair was twisted into its customary bun, tucked beneath a black bowler cap.

She waited in the narrow alley between two buildings, hidden from the street by wooden crates and other refuse. The building where Hamlet had taken Arhyen was only two blocks away, but she'd promised Ephraim she'd wait for him before going in.

A slight scuffle caught her ear, like the sound of a loafer lightly hissing across the asphalt.

"What exactly do you think you're doing?" a cultured voice inquired, his speech oddly broken.

Liliana stuffed her heart back down her throat, then turned her head to see Hamlet standing beside her, his white mask partially hidden in eerie shadows beneath his low top hat.

When she did not speak, he continued, "It would

seem you're considering seeking out Mr. Croft, when you had previously assured me you would not."

"It's been two weeks," she breathed. "I must know that he's alright."

Hamlet turned his gaze past her toward the open street beyond, as if drawn by movement, but seconds later he simply returned his gaze to her without comment. When she offered no further explanation, he replied, "I assure you he is alive and well."

"Then why has he not been returned to us?" she demanded. "Is it because of what he knows? What if they never release him?"

He snickered. "Which question would you like me to answer first?"

"The first one," she replied instantly, realizing she'd been blabbering.

"He has not been returned because the LN is searching for me," he explained. "And *you*."

She frowned. "Well, *I'm* not difficult to find. They already know everything about me."

Hamlet snickered again. "No *I* know everything about you. They do not even know if you still live, nor do they realize you are Mr. Croft's associate."

She shook her head, growing impatient as Ephraim would likely arrive soon, and Hamlet tended to disappear whenever she wasn't alone. "You lied before then. You said the LN wanted me."

He inclined his head. "That was no lie, and they still do, but fortunately I found you first, and I will not let them have you. Neither will Mr. Croft, judging by the fact that they have not apprehended you or Mr. Godwin."

"You mean he's refusing to tell them about us?" she asked, but before he could answer, she went on, "That's why you didn't let Ephraim and I walk you all the way to the building. We've only interacted with one of the LN's splinter groups. The *actual* organization doesn't know we're all working together."

"You're quite astute," he observed. "I really don't know why you ask questions at all."

"It helps me think," she answered honestly, "and even if I'm observant, some things I cannot divine without assistance."

Footsteps sounded on the empty street beyond the alleyway.

Before she could think better of it, her hand darted to Hamlet's wrist, grasping tightly, hoping to prevent his usual quick escape.

The pale eyes behind his mask widened, but he did not pull away. "I wasn't leaving," he explained, a hint of amusement in his voice.

She slowly retracted her hand. "Oh, I thought-"

He turned his gaze toward the open street, interrupting her words.

"*Liliana*," a voice hissed.

"Over here, Mr. Godwin," Hamlet announced.

Seeming to recognize Hamlet's voice, Ephraim muttered several choice expletives under his breath, then squeezed himself into the alleyway, weaving around the stacked crates and refuse piles.

Hamlet leaned close to her ear. "I'm not leaving you until I have your vow that you will not go after Mr. Croft," he whispered to her as Ephraim approached, still muttering under his breath.

She turned and narrowed her gaze at him, fighting the fear that hid in her stomach whenever she was near Hamlet. "You will not have it."

"To go after him now would endanger us all," he assured more loudly as Ephraim reached them.

"And why is that?" Ephraim enquired, having heard Hamlet's last statement. "And what are you doing here?"

"Preventing you from ruining everything," Hamlet replied. "As I've just finished explaining to Ms. Breckinridge, the London Network knows less about either of you than I have let on. To reveal yourselves now would not only endanger your lives, but Mr. Croft's. They have neglected to release him due to my disappearance. They are hoping that he will lead them to each of *you,* and perhaps others, and you will in turn lead them to *me*."

"So you're saying they're holding Arhyen because they want *you*," Ephraim stated bluntly, readjusting his fedora. "I believe the answer to our problems is for us to turn you in to them."

Hamlet chuckled. "And you believe you will be left alive afterward without me to protect you?"

Ephraim glared daggers at Hamlet, apparently not appreciating the implication that he needed protection.

"Well if you're so all-powerful," Ephraim replied, "then why don't you rescue Arhyen right this moment? It shouldn't be a difficult task for you."

Hamlet sighed. "Getting in would not be difficult. Escaping without Mr. Croft coming to harm is another matter."

"Then how did you plan on returning him to us?" Ephraim demanded before Liliana could.

Her head was beginning to spin. Had Hamlet known the LN would hold Arhyen prisoner all along, and if so, why did he bring him to their facility?

"He *will* be returned, I assure you," Hamlet replied. "I have a plan. I only ask for three more days."

"And what is your plan?" Ephraim asked, not missing a beat.

Hamlet took a step back.

Liliana wondered if he was trying to place himself out of her reach.

"That will be revealed in time," Hamlet explained. "For now, I assure you that going into that building tonight will only result in death for both you and Mr. Croft, and possibly worse for Ms. Breckinridge."

He took another step back into the shadows, and Liliana knew just what he was going to do before he did it. Almost too fast for the eye to see, he turned tail and ran.

She turned her worried gaze to Ephraim, quite sure they would not be seeing Hamlet again until whatever plan he'd concocted was at hand.

"Let's get you home," he sighed.

"But-" she began, not sure what argument she would make. Arhyen was so close, but according to Hamlet, if she attempted to rescue him, she would only be endangering his life. She couldn't risk it.

Fighting back tears, she nodded and led the way out of the alley. Ephraim followed, walking silently beside her the entire way home. In her panic to obtain information from Hamlet, she'd entirely forgotten about the mystery of the Captain of the Watch, in which Hamlet was deeply involved. He probably knew exactly what the blue liquid was, and now she and Ephraim would be left to try and figure it out on their own.

Fortunately, Ephraim was at least gracious enough to not mention her mistake, if it was even currently on his thoughts at all.

Arhyen had gone the entire night without seeing a soul. Apparently Wakefield's departure had signaled the start of his solitary confinement. He hadn't even been given an evening meal . . . not that he had much appetite.

He paced around the confines of his small room, going over everything Wakefield had told him. Even *if* Wakefield was the Captain of the Queen's Guard, Arhyen wasn't about to tell him about Liliana. It was almost a relief that the LN seemed to lack information he'd assumed they already possessed. Had Hamlet really protected them? If so, for what purpose? He couldn't help but think that it was some elaborate scheme that would end in all of their deaths.

The door's exterior lock slid open with a loud *clank*, drawing his attention seconds before the door swung inward, admitting Wakefield and two black-clad cronies, different men than before.

Wakefield smoothed an aged hand over his gray hair as he entered, though not a strand stood out of place. Arhyen hated to think what his shaggy brown hair might look like at this point. The small adjoining bathroom didn't have a mirror, likely a preventative to him obtaining any sharp objects.

Arhyen remained standing as the chair was moved across the room, then waited silently as Wakefield took his seat. Then, he waited some more.

Wakefield observed his fingernails as if they were the most interesting thing in the world. His cronies waited silently behind him, gazes trained on the opposite wall above Arhyen's bed.

Arhyen crossed his arms, refusing to be the first to speak.

Finally, Wakefield lowered his hand and met Arhyen's gaze. "Have you considered my offer?"

Arhyen remained silent.

Wakefield snorted. "I see you are a fool after all."

Arhyen smirked. "I would be a fool to believe you will just let me walk out of here with what I know. Automatons created to be weapons, humans experimented on to become more like the aforementioned automatons." He stopped himself before he could mention the synthetic emotions created by Fairfax Breckinridge. They likely weren't aware he knew about that, and such information might lead them to search for Liliana.

"The group who kidnapped you was no longer part of the London Network," Wakefield corrected gruffly. "We do not condone human experimentation."

Arhyen saw no purpose to pointing out the lie. Just because Hazel had branched off to continue experiments on her own, did not mean the technology hadn't originated within the London Network. *Someone* had turned Hazel into what she was long before she went into business for herself.

Wakefield stood. "I am prepared to offer not only your safety, but the safety of your associates, minus Codename Hamlet, of course, in return for information."

Arhyen shook his head. "Like I said, I don't believe for a second that I will remain among the living after you find Hamlet. I'd rather only *my* death be on my hands."

Wakefield's expression contorted with rage seconds before he swatted his chair, sending it clattering across the room. "You realize you're protecting a terrorist!" he growled. "You're endangering the lives of all within this great city!"

He tried to keep his expression calm in the face of such sudden fury. He supposed Hamlet could easily be considered a terrorist, but he'd been working *for* the LN. Surely they were the ones accountable for his actions.

"What do you mean, terrorist?" he questioned finally.

Seeming to calm himself, Wakefield retrieved his chair and resumed his seat.

Sensing an opportunity for more information, Arhyen finally sat on his bed, facing Wakefield.

"Codename Hamlet was created a long time ago," Wakefield began. "I only learned of his existence after many years of service to the Queen. Though all I really knew was that he worked *for* us, not against us. Recently, it was brought to my attention that he was no longer obeying orders. He was not just eliminating the splinter groups of our organization, but loyal members. We also believe he's hiding potentially devastating information, and planning something that will mean ruin for us all."

A million thoughts flitted through Arhyen's mind, though chief amongst them were Fairfax's synthetic emotions. Did the LN actually possess the formulae now, like Hamlet had led them to believe, or had he kept them for his own purposes? He couldn't very well ask in case they were unaware of the matter.

"What makes you believe he's planning something?" he asked instead.

Wakefield laced his hands together, then leaned forward, elbows balanced on knees. "Destruction of evidence, top secret files going missing . . . hidden associates," he added with a stern look for Arhyen. "The list goes on. He's hiding something. Those who last interacted with him believe he's gone mad, which is likely. To our knowledge, no automaton has been allowed to survive for anywhere near as long as he has. Most are remanufactured every few years to prevent any . . . *malfunctions*. Truly, it doesn't matter if he's mad, or plotting, or both. He's capable of great destruction, and has managed to elude us now for weeks. Even once we manage to locate him, he will be difficult to destroy."

Arhyen frowned. "So, in other words, the London Network created its own problems, and now rather than dealing with them yourselves, you've roped me into this whole fiasco."

His anger returning as abruptly as it had the first time, Wakefield stood. "The London Network saved your life, young man, and you should not be naive enough to think we don't know just who you are. Arhyen Croft, born into poverty, climbing the ladder rungs of the underground as a thief. You should be rotting in prison right now, not receiving medical care and offers of protection."

Arhyen smirked. "I almost did rot in prison thanks to *your* corrupt Captain of the Watch."

"How did you know about that?" Wakefield gasped.

"I know a lot of things," Arhyen replied, rising from the bed to hover over Wakefield's shorter form, "and you are correct, I am not naive enough to think you don't know just who I am, therefore I am not naive enough to believe my life in any way matters to you. If you want my help, we are going to play by *my* rules, else I'll gladly sit here while Hamlet burns London to the ground."

Wakefield opened his mouth then shut it several times, his eyes bugging out of their sockets. Finally, he seemed to gather himself. "What do you propose?"

"I propose you provide me with *leverage*," he replied, quickly formulating a plan. "Give me top secret information that I will provide to certain *associates* that should I die, will be released to the public on a grand scale, but as long as I live, the information will remain unknown."

Wakefield puffed up his chest and bristled his moustache. "You would like the London Network to entrust valuable information to a common thief, trusting on his word alone that it will not be spread regardless if you live or die?"

"Do you want help locating Hamlet before he enacts his dastardly plan, or not?"

Wakefield's face grew increasingly red as he seemed to genuinely consider Arhyen's proposal.

Honestly, he'd just been testing the man. He hadn't believed in a thousand years that his deal would be accepted.

"I will discuss this with my superiors," Wakefield said finally, then turned on his heel and marched out of the room, followed by his cronies, just as currently red-faced and bug-eyed as he.

As the door shut behind them, Arhyen slumped onto his bed with a sigh. Life as a thief never could have prepared him for offering ultimatums to the alleged Captain of the Queen's Guard. Nor could it stop his heart from hammering at the slim chance that he might actually live to see Liliana again. He would not hesitate to take her in his arms and kiss her, though he was afraid once he did, he would never let her go.

CHAPTER 3

Liliana awoke the next morning with a groan. Though she wasn't overly affected by the cold, her foggy breath signaled that the apartment had turned into an ice cave. She pulled the blanket up over her face, strongly considering staying in bed all day. She had no desire to further test the mysterious blue liquid, but other than that, she had absolutely nothing to do. Ephraim would be working through their normal noontime meeting that day, and Hamlet wasn't likely to show himself before his three days were up.

She threw aside the blanket and lowered her feet to the floor. There had to be *something* she could do. She rubbed her bleary eyes as she glanced around the small apartment. Except for the pile of evidence on the low table, there wasn't a speck of dust or mess anywhere. After years of tidying up after Fairfax Breckinridge, she tended to clean without realizing it. Since Arhyen had been gone and she'd had extra time, she'd cleaned the entire apartment top to bottom, even organizing

Arhyen's old trunks of clothing they occasionally used for disguises.

She padded across the cold floor toward the stove to prepare her morning tea. She'd taken to not eating much the past two weeks, as she didn't really need food, and it wasn't as fun to consume without Arhyen around, but she still enjoyed her tea. It seemed to help her think. Perhaps it would help her think of something to do to occupy her time.

Reaching the stove next to the short countertop and sink, she filled the kettle and lit the flame. Ten minutes later she found herself on the sofa, with a nice cup of hot tea in hand, wearing her comfortable stealthy clothes since she didn't plan on seeing anyone soon.

Her eyes scanned the evidence on the table, all covered in that bright blue substance, the composition of which still eluded her. Taking a sip of her tea, she rifled through the facts in her mind.

The day after the Captain confessed to his crimes, his home had been searched for additional evidence. Ephraim, newly reinstated as a detective after his erroneous arrest, had been involved in the search. According to him, the blue stains had still been in liquid form, moist and sticky to the touch. Unfortunately, the detectives had all worn gloves, so they had no experimental evidence as to what the liquid might do if touched when fresh.

She took another sip of her tea. That the liquid was still fresh at least told her it likely had something to do with the Captain's confession, since it must have been spilled right before he went to Watch Headquarters to turn himself in. Could it be some sort of truth serum? Such a thing existed in her novels, but not in real life . . . that she knew of. Yet, if it was a truth serum, he could have simply avoided Watch Headquarters until its effects wore off. The story went that he marched right in that morning and confessed his crimes without any prompting.

That led her to believe it was due to mind control, though that once again was only part of the fictional worlds she liked to read about. Perhaps she was making things too complicated. It really could just be ink.

She frowned and set her half-empty teacup on the table. If it was mere ink, why did it contain human cells? Perhaps that should be her starting point. Of course, the only use for human cells she could think of was the creation of automatons, and that made little sense regarding this case. It had to be something else.

She leaned forward and started shuffling through the various stained papers and other articles. That was the other thing that didn't make sense. There was so much mess. Had there been some sort of struggle, spilling the liquid everywhere? She'd love to ask the Captain himself, but he'd gone conveniently mute after his confession, refusing to speak to anyone, even those who knew him best.

Her thoughts trailed off. She was repeating herself. She'd gone over all this before, and it still made no sense. She was missing something.

That something was likely Hamlet. She knew he was in some way involved with the Captain's confession. If only she had thought to ask him the previous night. Now she had no way of finding him.

She pursed her lips and leaned back against the lumpy sofa cushion. Perhaps that last thought wasn't entirely true. He'd somehow known she was going to attempt Arhyen's rescue, so either he was watching her, or he'd assigned others to the task. That meant if she wanted to see him again, all she had to do was draw him out.

Her resolve strengthened, she stood, then walked to one of the clothing chests where she'd draped her magenta dress the day before. If she was going out during the day she'd need to blend in, and that meant dressing like a *lady*. Staring down at the dress, she tsked. She'd much rather be one of the women in her novels, exploring mysterious tombs in Egypt, or braving the Amazon in search of hidden treasure. Not sipping tea in a shop in a frilly dress and matching hat, oblivious to the secret organization running London.

With a sigh, she took her garment to the bathroom to change.

Soon she was prim and proper in her modest gown, her neck and wrists demurely covered. Her hair was in its customary bun, though no hat bedecked her vibrant red tresses.

Feeling a thrill of excitement at her mission, she rushed around the apartment, equipping her handbag with throwing daggers and a few smoke bombs, just in case. She paused beside the low coffee table in thought, then plucked a small piece of stained paper from its surface, folding it in two before stuffing it in her bag. Finished, she left the apartment, locking the door behind her.

The sky outside was gray, and there was a crispness to the air, promising snow. It would be her first snow since she came to live in the city, a thought that caused her an odd feeling of heartache since she'd be experiencing it alone.

Shaking her emotions away, she clutched her handbag firmly with one hand, then lifted the hem of her skirts with the other before taking off at a jog.

Taking a left at the first narrow intersection, her mind shuffled through the places she might go where

Hamlet was likely to find her. Her first thought was the building where Arhyen was being held, but after Hamlet's warning, she feared being seen by someone other than him. She didn't want to risk Arhyen's life simply to draw Hamlet out. Her next thought was London Bridge. Would he attempt to stop her if she left the city?

She slowed her pace as she neared the main thoroughfare of Market Street. It would be a shame if she traveled all the way out of the city, only to have him not reveal himself.

Two gentlemen in frock coats and short top hats eyed her up and down as they walked past. At first she thought she should probably be offended, then realized the looks may have been garnered because she'd paused in the middle of the sidewalk, deep in thought, oblivious to those attempting to pass her.

She picked up her pace, hoping to not draw any extra attention to herself. She hurried past the various cafes and other businesses, ignoring the odd pangs of memory that accosted her, especially when she passed the shop where she'd had her first slice of chocolate cake, the morning after she'd followed Arhyen out of her father's hidden compound. She realized sadly that she was beginning to believe she'd never see Arhyen again. What if Hamlet's plan went awry, and he was not able to deliver on his promises? What if he never meant to keep them in the first place?

She lifted her hands to her lips, remembering the kiss she'd shared with Arhyen. She'd never imagined that such a thing could happen to her, but now that it had, she could not let the feeling go, even if it was a feeling she didn't fully understand.

Her steps slowed as another familiar storefront came into view. She looked up and read the sign, *Flowers of*

Antimony. Why hadn't she thought of this sooner? Last she'd seen, Victor Ashdown's daughter, Chirani, had been running his alchemy shop. What if this new, brightly-hued compound was something else he'd left behind like his electricity stones? Chirani might be able to tell her what she was dealing with, and she wouldn't need to find Hamlet that day after all.

With a new spring in her step, she approached the storefront and peered through the glass. Sure enough, Chirani was within, mixing something in a large bowl behind the counter. Her dark skin and exotic features contrasted beautifully with the simple lilac dress she wore, though her expression seemed troubled. Perhaps because her father had never been officially pronounced dead. Liliana grimaced. Or maybe it was because she had never returned to notify Chirani of such news as promised.

Suddenly anxious, she opened the shop door, which announced her with a cheerful jingle. Chirani looked up from her work in question, then smiled. Liliana hurried forward, feeling encouraged by Chirani's expression.

"I'd thought perhaps you'd left the city when I didn't see you again," Chirani admitted, stepping away from her work.

With a smile, Liliana approached the counter and set her handbag down, though she did not yet withdraw the stained paper. "I apologize for not visiting sooner. I know I assured you I'd let you know if I found anything out about your father, but I never did."

Chirani frowned and shook her head. "I've lost hope in those regards. If he was still alive, he would have returned by now, or at the very least, would have found some way to send me word. I'm not naive enough to believe that my father told me all his secrets, but he wouldn't let me worry all this time if he was still around."

Liliana nodded, wondering how much she should tell her. She deserved to know the truth, but certain information could be dangerous. She didn't want to risk making Chirani a target. "I believe he's dead as well," she declared with a sad sigh. "An associate of mine claimed he'd heard of his death, though I was unable to recover the exact details."

She felt guilty at the small lie, but she couldn't quite bring herself to tell Chirani her father had been tortured and killed by Clayton Blackwood, and that his body was likely rotting in a sewer, or perhaps had been burned to ash. Clayton was dead now, murdered by Hamlet, so at the very least, justice had been served.

With a sad smile, Chirani nodded, accepting Liliana's explanation. "As I said, I suspected as much, but I appreciate you coming here to tell me what you know."

"There's something else," she added, making a snap decision. She reached into her handbag and withdrew the sheet of paper with its incriminating blue stain. "Do you know what this is?"

Chirani took the offered paper and peered down at the stain, then raised her eyes to meet Liliana's. "Ink?"

Liliana's shoulders slumped in disappointment. Perhaps not a creation of Victor Ashdown's after all.

"Why is this of interest to you?" Chirani questioned, handing back the paper.

She clenched her jaw, reluctant to tell another lie, though she knew she had no choice. The entire city had heard of the Captain's confession, but his crimes were still under investigation.

She tucked the paper back within her handbag. "A friend asked me to look into it," she explained. "He seems to think it is something other than ink," she hesitated, "and it contains human cells."

Rather than showing signs of shock, Chirani furrowed her brow in thought. "Human cells, you say?" she muttered. "I wonder if it has anything to do with creating automatons." Her distant gaze became more clear as it turned back to Liliana. "I unfortunately know little about *that* aspect of alchemy, though my father was always intrigued by them."

"Them?" Liliana questioned.

"Automatons," Chirani clarified. "He was never involved in creating them, but he did research."

That didn't come as a surprise to Liliana. Victor had created the *Advector Serum* used to grant her human emotions, after all. Though she couldn't say so out loud, as Chirani didn't even know she was an automaton. She'd likely not speak so freely with her if she found out.

"I'd considered that the liquid might be an aspect of growing artificial life," Liliana replied finally, "but it doesn't necessarily make sense with where this liquid was found."

Chirani arched a dark brow. "And where was it found?" she asked suspiciously.

She blinked up at her, furiously attempting to concoct a lie that would make sense. She was saved by someone knocking on the storefront glass behind her.

Chirani peered in the direction of the sound. "There's a rather strange man attempting to get your attention."

Liliana turned, half-expecting to see Hamlet, but what she got was Wilfred Morris, known thug for hire, and also someone she and Ephraim had questioned several weeks ago in relation to the LN. Wilfred had allegedly been hired by the LN to smuggle goods through the canals, only to have his employers knock him over the skull, leaving him for dead in a remote waterway.

Upon gaining her attention, Wilfred waved.

She turned back to Chirani, wondering what she could possibly say to explain the burly, scarred thug waiting outside her shop. "M-my cousin," she blurted. "He occasionally escorts me to see that I don't find myself in trouble. He must have grown impatient with waiting."

Chirani's eyes were narrowed in suspicion, but she nodded. "Well, I hope to see you again. I will search through my father's books to see if I can find anything out about your mysterious blue liquid."

Liliana smiled in relief. "I would appreciate that."

With a final wave, she hurried out of the shop to meet Wilfred.

He waited just long enough for the door to shut behind her, then started walking along the streetside.

She hurried to catch up to him. "Did you follow me here?" she whispered, wondering at his sudden appearance. He hadn't seemed a particularly bad man when she met him, but he was also a criminal. She'd put nothing past him.

He raked his meaty palm through his short, roughly-cut brown hair. "Nah. I was attending other business when I caught sight of your hair. Did the information I gave you ever pan out to anything?"

Liliana took a moment to observe him. His brow was covered in a sickly sweat, and his blue eyes darted from side to side. "Why are you so nervous?" she questioned softly, debating running off the other way.

He stopped walking and pulled her into a nearby alleyway. Reacting instantly, her fingers darted into her handbag for a dagger, but as soon as they were in the alley, he released her and stepped back.

"Sorry for that," he muttered, glancing warily at her hand in her bag. "You never know who might be listenin'." He walked further into the alley.

With a quick glance over her shoulder, Liliana followed.

He stopped a few paces away and waited for her to catch up. "Truth be told, I've been on the look out for you, or for one of the chaps you're usually with. Something bad is brewin', and I'm starting to worry that it might have been unwise for me to give you information."

She frowned. "The-" she stopped herself before she could say *London Network* out loud. "*Those* people tried to kill you," she said out loud. "You cannot be blamed for desiring retribution."

He glanced nervously at the nearby street and its carefree people. "Retribution won't mean nothin' if I'm dead. Word is there's a masked man going around the underworld, killing anyone who's ever been involved with the LN. I should have never opened my mouth."

Liliana's eyes widened. Did he mean Hamlet? She quickly tried to conceal her expression, but it was too late.

Wilfred's mouth hung open in realization. "You know something, don't you? Something about this masked killer?"

She blinked at him, unsure what to say. She wanted to tell him he would be fine, but she couldn't guarantee that she could find Hamlet and ask him not to kill Wilfred, and even if she could, she couldn't guarantee that he would listen.

"I have repeated what you told me to no one," she

said instead. "As long as you told no one else, you should be fine."

"I told plenty of people!" he hissed. "That was how your detective friend found me to begin with," he continued in hushed tones. "I filed a report with the Watch. It's on record!"

She took a deep breath. "Try to calm down," she instructed. "You don't even know if these rumors are true."

He shook his head. "They're true, and I'm going to be next. Your detective friend has to help me. Lock me in a jail cell for all I care."

"I'm sorry," she breathed. "I don't know what I can do to help you."

Clearly in a panic, he took a step toward her.

She didn't think he would attack, but given his size and frenzied state, she felt nervous. She had her automaton speed and strength, daggers, and smoke bombs, but she didn't want to hurt the poor man.

"You have to help me," he pleaded, taking another step toward her in the narrow alley.

She stepped back again and her shoulders hit the wall. She tensed, ready to run.

Wilfred took another step toward her, one massive hand outstretched, while the other reached into his coat pocket. His movements halted as something hit the side of his neck with a *thwack*. He blinked in confusion, lowered his arms, then slumped to the ground, a dagger protruding from the side of his throat, piercing the large artery.

Liliana raised a hand to her lips to stifle her scream. A hand touched her shoulder, causing her to jump. She peeled her gaze away from the puddle of blood slowly growing beneath Wilfred to find Hamlet had silently appeared at her side. He withdrew his hand from her shoulder at her horrified look.

"Why did you kill him?" she hissed, the first tears escaping her eyes. The poor man had been terrified. He'd only wanted help.

"He was about to attack you," Hamlet replied simply, "and I was too far down the alley to prevent him by force."

She glared at him through her tears. "Your hearing is just as good as mine. You heard him asking for my help."

"Indeed," Hamlet agreed, then looked down at Wilfred. "I also saw him reaching for the knife in his pocket."

Liliana turned her gaze back to Wilfred in surprise. The hand he'd reached into his pocket still remained. Hamlet kicked Wilfred's limp arm with the toe of his boot. The hand came free, and a shiny silver knife clattered from his pocket to the cobblestones.

"B-but why?" she stammered, turning her gaze back to Hamlet. "He said he was afraid the LN was after him and wanted my help. Why would he draw a knife?"

His eyes remained on Wilfred. "I'm not entirely sure. I heard him mention a masked man. Perhaps he was fishing for information on my whereabouts."

Liliana shook her head, still not understanding. "But why?"

"Because the London Network is looking for me," he explained. "They seem quite desperate for information at this point. They seem to think I'm planning something."

She turned her gaze up to him. "But you *are* planning something."

He inclined his head. "Yes, I am. Would you allow me to escort you home?"

Liliana looked back down at the dead body, feeling

sorry for him, even though he'd been preparing to attack her, perhaps to torture her for information. Instead, he'd facilitated drawing out Hamlet who now could walk her home. She could finally ask all of her questions . . . not that he'd necessarily answer them, but it was worth a try.

Her mind made up, she nodded. "I actually have something to show you," she admitted. "I'm hoping you might know what it is."

Curiosity glittered in the blue eyes behind his mask, just one of many emotions an automaton like Hamlet should not feel. She wished she could ask him every burning question stored within her clockwork heart, but some, perhaps, even he could not answer.

❧

THOUGH SHE HAD COUNTLESS QUESTIONS TO ASK, THE long silence drew out as Liliana walked by Hamlet's side, keeping to the back streets and alleyways leading back to Arhyen's apartment. She knew he'd been involved in the Watch Captain's confession, so what if he didn't want her looking into the blue liquid? Though she'd come to trust Hamlet to a degree, she still found him frightening. He was not like the humans she'd grown accustomed to. She couldn't depend on the driving forces of compassion and conscience in his decision making.

They weren't far off from the apartment now, which was fortunate. The sky seemed about ready to burst with either rain or snow. She could taste it on the air. Perhaps she'd just get Hamlet inside, allowing him to witness the blue stained articles strewn across the tabletop himself. Then, even if he said nothing, she could at least judge his reaction.

"You said you had something to show me?" he questioned, startling her out of her thoughts.

Their footfalls echoed lightly on the cobblestones, the sound bouncing off the nearby buildings lining either side of the narrow walkway. They seemed deafeningly loud to her as she strained her hearing to pick up any possible eavesdroppers.

"Yes," she said finally. She could have pulled the stained piece of paper out of her handbag right then, but something compelled her not to. Perhaps she wanted to trap him in the apartment so he couldn't just run off without answering.

He didn't comment further, and instead remained silently at her side until they reached the apartment door. She fished one of the keys out of her handbag, unlocking one set of locks, then retrieved a second key for the others. Hamlet watched on curiously like a tall, dark shadow at her side.

Soon enough she opened the door and stepped inside, instructing Hamlet to step over the tripwire as he entered. She shut the door behind him, then leaned against it, exhaling in an odd mixture of relief and apprehension.

Though it could only be around four or five in the evening, the apartment was dark. The building clouds outside provided only the barest hint of light through the curtained window.

Not seeming to notice, Hamlet stepped around the sofa to peer down at the low table. "Ah," he began, his tone unreadable. "Now I understand."

"S-so you recognize it?" she questioned, stepping away from the closed door.

He shrugged, the gesture minimized by his heavy black coat. "Perhaps."

She took a shaky breath, then moved around the sofa to the opposite end of the table. She looked up to meet his shadowed gaze. "Perhaps?"

He snorted, and she imagined him smirking beneath his mask. "You are well aware that the more information you know, the more danger you are in."

"A man just tried to stab me in an alleyway," she joked half-heartedly. "I'm already in danger."

He gave a slight nod, then began to pace around the table.

She quickly hopped back out of the way.

He trailed his gloved fingers across the top end of the microscope, then leaned down to riffle through a few of the stained papers. "What have you learned thus far?" he questioned, straightening as he turned to face her.

She bit her lip, unsure of how much she should say. She had a feeling he was testing her, as Ephraim often did.

"It contains human biological material," she replied softly. "That is all I have deduced."

"Hmph," he replied, then turned away, pacing further around the table.

She was beginning to regret inviting him in. He obviously wasn't going to give her any answers, and now he was just making her nervous.

He suddenly stopped and turned toward her again. "If I tell you, I cannot allow you to relay the information to Mr. Godwin."

She frowned, caught off guard by the request. "Why ever not?"

"You are already aware of the need to prevent certain information from spreading," he explained. "The research of Fairfax Breckinridge, for example."

"Is this my father's work?" she asked in surprise, gesturing down at the table.

He shook his head. "It is the London Network's creation, actually. Part of the reason for my plan. Men need to learn that certain things should be left up to fate alone."

She stared at him, but he didn't seem to notice her. He seemed lost somewhere deep within his mind.

Suddenly, he seemed to snap back into awareness. "I would not research this further, if I were you."

"Why?" she blurted without thinking. "What is your plan?"

He finished his path around the table, walking past her as if he would head toward the door. Instead, he paused and landed a hand on her shoulder. "Anyone who associates with me is currently in danger. I recommend you stay in hiding until my time is up. Just two more days."

"But-" she began, confused by his cryptic statement.

"No buts," he interrupted, his hand still on her shoulder. "I will return Mr. Croft to you, for what it's worth."

"For what it's worth?" she asked weakly.

He sighed. "You'll learn in time that we simply cannot be human, no matter how much we *feel*."

She turned her head slightly to peer up at him. "I thought you didn't *feel*," she stated bluntly.

"I don't," he replied, confusion in his blue eyes. "I think, perhaps, I've been around too long, and I'm simply going mad."

She inhaled sharply. She'd thought from time to time that perhaps Hamlet was entirely mad, but to hear him say so was still shocking. Wasn't part of being mad not knowing it?

He dropped his hand from her shoulder. "Please, stay inside, Liliana." He left her and headed toward the door.

Recovering from her surprise, she hurried to follow him. He still hadn't answered what the blue liquid was, nor had he explained the nature of his plan. She'd learned nothing.

She reached the door just as he opened it and stepped outside. She opened her mouth to ask all her questions, but then he turned, stopping her with the pained look in his eyes. Pain he wasn't supposed to feel.

He looked up as the first white, fluffy flakes began to fall in the dimming daylight. "I always liked the snow," he commented softly, then turned and walked away.

Liliana stared out the open door for a long while after he left. The snow continued to fall, blanketing the outside world in white. She eyed the serene scene, Hamlet's words lingering in her mind, reiterating nearly the same thing her father had said to her in a letter. *She could never be human, no matter how much she felt.*

It brought to her mind a question she didn't want to consider, but it came forward none-the-less. If being an automaton for so long had driven Hamlet mad, was she next?

CHAPTER 4

Arhyen waited patiently while an older woman in a white medical coat checked over his healing incisions. Her graying hair, pulled back into a tight bun, accentuated her stern features, inviting no conversation.

A full day had passed since he had spoken to Wakefield, or anyone else for that matter. At least, he thought it had been a full day. The electric lights in his room had customarily dimmed, signaling that night had fallen, and he'd awoken as soon as they brightened, but for all he knew, they were shortening his days as a psychological tactic, breaking him down by making him think he'd been there for more days than he actually had. After all he'd learned about the LN thus far, he wouldn't be surprised.

Returning to her wheeled metal cart, the woman lifted a small pointed mallet and began testing his reflexes. She was utterly silent throughout the checkup, just as she had been on previous visits.

He eyed the cart while she tapped the mallet against

each of his knees. There didn't appear to be much he could use upon it, and the armed guards near the door let him know with their cold gazes that thievery would not be tolerated.

He flinched as the woman suddenly jabbed him with a needle, withdrawing yet more blood.

"You know," he groaned, "I don't believe this vial of blood will be any different from all the others."

"Then you apparently know nothing," she replied, surprising him. Her gaze remained on the vial, slowly filling with crimson.

"Do go on," he pressed.

She withdrew the needle and capped it before setting it on her little table, then she crouched to a bottom shelf on the wheeled cart and retrieved a stack of bound papers. She tossed them to him as she stood.

He was so surprised he almost didn't manage to catch them. He looked down at the neatly printed pages, then back up at the woman.

"I'm told that we are now sharing information with you, though I do not know why," she explained. "Acquaint yourself with the materials. Captain Wakefield will visit you tomorrow morning."

With that, she pushed her little cart out of the room, followed by the two guards.

He stared at the door as it shut behind them. Had his plan actually worked? He'd only been throwing out ideas to keep Wakefield talking, but apparently something had stuck. He wasn't free yet, but if they were sharing information with him, it was a start.

He looked down at the bound packet of papers in his hand, his eye immediately drawn to his name printed in bold letters across the top.

He sighed. Perhaps he'd gotten his hopes up too soon,

and they were simply showing him all the information they'd gathered on *him*.

Not expecting much, he turned to the next page. He skimmed down through the text, not understanding half of what he was reading, but it soon became clear that he was holding not his criminal case file, but his *medical* file. Listed within were all of the operations he'd undergone, and all the LN had done to stabilize him.

He felt ill as he scanned through to the next page. Were any of his organs truly his anymore? Hazel hadn't been careful about what she did to him.

Unable to read the gory details, he flipped to the next page, finding the notes covering his ongoing status: blood and reflex tests, physical observations, *everything*. Intrigued by what his examiner had alluded to about his blood not being the same blood every time it was drawn, he honed in on those results, but they were not written in terminology he understood. He could, however, see that the results had changed over time. What could it mean? Was his body still changing as a result of Hazel's experimentations?

He continued to flip through the pages, but half of it was gibberish to him, and the other half he wasn't sure he wanted to know. He placed the packet on his bedside table, then slumped back onto his pillow to stare at the ceiling. His *blood* was changing, but why? Would there be other physical changes soon to come?

His arms erupted in goosebumps as he thought back to Hazel's madness. Did the same fate await him? If she'd done similar things to him as what had been done to her, it stood to reason that he'd end up in the same place.

He rolled onto his side, then snatched the packet of papers from the small table, determined to make sense of them. He hated to admit it, but perhaps he shouldn't escape the LN right away, as much as he wanted to. They might very well be the only ones who could save him, and should things go awry, he knew they would not hesitate to put an end to him.

A grim thought, but sometimes grim thoughts were necessary, especially when one had potentially been made into a monster.

❦

LILIANA STARED AT THE CEILING STREAKED WITH RAYS of early morning light streaming in through the nearby window. She'd stayed inside as Hamlet had requested, and now another night was lost.

She turned on her side and pulled the blanket up over her face, then groaned as a knock sounded at the door. She wasn't expecting visitors. Had Catherine perhaps returned to see if she would offer help? She hoped not. With everything else going on, she'd completely forgotten about Catherine's predicament. Of course, now that Hamlet was no longer associating with the LN, there would be nothing she could do for Catherine. She'd have to find gainful employment somewhere else.

She stumbled out of bed and quickly donned a coat over her white shift before hurrying to the door. She climbed onto her stool and peered through the peephole, exhaling in relief to see Ephraim waiting outside.

She quickly hopped to the ground, moved her stool, and turned all the locks before opening the door.

Before she could say anything, Ephraim strode inside. "The Captain of the Watch is dead," he announced, turning toward her. "There were no signs of foul play or self-harm. He is simply dead, and now we may never solve the case behind his confession."

Liliana glanced outside, noting the cobblestones damp with melting snow, then slowly closed the door. Sighing, she leaned against it. "Dead?" she questioned, waiting for her thoughts to catch up to her.

"Quite," Ephraim replied.

She sighed and turned a few of the locks on the door before tightening the sash of her long coat. Sufficiently covered, she walked past Ephraim toward the sofa and sat. She then waited patiently for him to join her, which he did with a huff of exasperation, removing his fedora as he sat.

"I questioned Hamlet about the blue liquid," she explained, "but all I managed to learn was that it was created by the London Network. He advised I not look into it further."

Ephraim narrowed his pale eyes at her. "And you intend to follow this advice?"

"No," she replied after a moment's hesitation, "but my thoughts are currently preoccupied with what will happen in two day's time." She frowned. "Actually, it was two more days yesterday, which could mean that Hamlet's plan may come to fruition as early as midnight tonight, or as late as midnight tomorrow, depending on how you look at it."

Ephraim shook his head, biting his lip in a rare show of frustration. "We must learn of his plan by midnight then. We simply cannot trust that all will be well. Too many have died already."

She waited for him to go on, but he remained silent, still chewing on his lip. Something about the Captain's death had riled him, and he was not easily riled. He'd seen far worse than a single death in the past month, so what could it be?

She waited patiently for several more seconds, then

cleared her throat. "Was there something in particular about the Captain's death that has upset you?"

He seemed to startle, then turned to glare at her. "I'm *not* upset."

She raised an eyebrow, then glanced down at his hands, gripping his knees painfully tight. "Clearly not."

He sighed, then released his knees. "Christoph, the Captain, was someone I once considered a friend. He was the reason I've remained a detective for as long as I have, after various . . . infractions."

She furrowed her brow. "But he framed you for murder."

Ephraim nodded as his gaze went distant. "Yes, precisely why I'd like to get to the bottom of this. Framing me, I can understand. We all fear death to varying degrees, but most of us don't see it coming. He knew his death was imminent, and he did what he had to do to prevent it. But the confession . . . " he trailed off, then shook his head. "The confession I do not understand. He would not go to such great lengths to save his own life, only to give it up, and knowing he had nothing else to lose, he would not have allowed anyone to threaten him into confessing."

Liliana was beginning to see his point. She'd thought the confession odd from the start, but had speculated that perhaps the Captain had been struck by conscience. With the new information, she did not think that the case. A man who would frame not only his colleague, but his long-time *friend* for murder did not have a conscience.

Seeming to see something encouraging in her expression, he continued, "Hamlet and this blue liquid *both* have something to do with his confession. While we do not know what Hamlet plans, I believe it's safe to assume it's something big. There will likely be risks, and if he dies along with Christoph, I fear we'll never have answers."

Liliana inhaled sharply. She truly hadn't considered the idea of Hamlet coming to harm. He seemed so . . . invincible. Yet, if his plan went awry and he ended up dead, what would become of Arhyen?

She stood abruptly. "I agree. We simply *must* find out what Hamlet is planning. Someone else has to know. A man tried to kill me yesterday based on my associations with him."

"A man tried to kill you!" he barked. "Why didn't you *start* with that? Here I've been blathering on about my suspicions-"

"I apologize," she interrupted. "Honestly, I had forgotten about it until now. It wasn't much of a scene. Hamlet dispatched him quickly."

Ephraim leaned forward in his seat, raising a hand to his brow as he shook his head. "Please," he began patiently, "when we have our meetings, please *lead* with such information."

Liliana rolled her eyes, then trotted across the apartment to fetch her dress. "Where will we go first?" she questioned over her shoulder, gathering the fabric in her arms. "I'm sure there's *someone* we could question. At the very least perhaps they'll try to kill us and Hamlet will appear again."

Seeming to regain his composure, Ephraim stood and tsked at her. "You can't depend on Hamlet's appearance every time someone tries to kill you."

She smirked. "I don't *depend* on it, but it *is* rather convenient when I'm trying to find him . . . " she trailed off as her thoughts suddenly jumped to another subject.

"You know it's frightening when you smile like that," Ephraim commented.

She chuckled. "My apologies, but I just realized who we can question first, or really, who we can *hire* to give us answers."

Ephraim scoffed. "My dear, I don't know if you realize this, but Arhyen has left you with very little coin."

She batted her eyelashes at him as she made her way toward the bathroom, her dress slung across her arm. "Who said we'd be spending *my* coin?"

He sighed and slumped back down onto the sofa. "At least tell me who we'll be hiring?"

"Arhyen's mother," she replied. She was about to seal herself within the bathroom, but hesitated. Ephraim would not want sympathy, but . . . "I'm sorry about your friend. Even after all that he put you through, I'm sure the loss is painful."

He glared at her for a moment, then his expression softened as he gave her a slight nod. He appreciated the sympathy, even though he would not acknowledge it further.

"Get your coin ready," she sighed, hoping to lighten the mood. "I'm sure Catherine does not come cheap."

She could hear Ephraim cursing as she shut the door behind her, but she hardly listened. She had a new direction, and she was prepared to run with it, especially now that she'd considered the dangers of what might happen after midnight.

One way or another, she needed to ensure Arhyen's safety, even if Hamlet's plans went up in flames in the process.

CHAPTER 5

"Tell me again *why* you have this woman's address?" Ephraim hissed as they crept toward the rundown building.

It was around noon, so the city was alive with the chatter of bustling ladies and steam horns, flavored with the scent of cooking food and baking bread. Liliana's mouth watered at the thought of a pastry from the nearby shop, but they had other matters to attend to.

Though the address Catherine had given her was two blocks west of Market Street, she and Ephraim were currently safe from the view of any onlookers. Only those looking for trouble traveled the backstreets, and most of those types tended to keep their eyes to themselves.

"She wanted me to put her in touch with Hamlet," Liliana muttered, scanning the building's roof for hidden threats.

"What is with that automaton?" Ephraim grumbled. "Suddenly he's the most popular man in London."

Assuming Ephraim's question was rhetoric, Liliana hurried forward, closing the distance to the heavy metal door of the building. It appeared to be a warehouse, with few windows, and dingy, gray-brick walls three times taller than any shop.

Ephraim followed closely behind her, then took the lead as they reached the door. He lifted his hand to knock, then seeming to think better of it, he tried the handle. The door opened inward with a long, metallic creak.

He poked his head into the shadowy interior, then withdrew it to look at Liliana. "Are you sure this is the correct address?"

She nodded. This was the address on the paper handed to her by Catherine. Always wary of a trap, Liliana held a finger to her lips to silence Ephraim, then leaned her head toward the open door.

He glared at her indignantly, but obeyed.

She strained to focus only on noises coming from within the building, but it was difficult with Market Street so near. Her hearing was much better than a human's, but because of that she often found herself distracted by ambient noise.

She stuck her head a little further into the dark building. She could hear the occasional scuffle of feet, and murmuring voices, all coming from one of the upper floors.

She withdrew her head. "There are people upstairs," she explained, looking up at Ephraim. "I can't say for sure how many, but I'd guess only four or five. They seem to be relaxed, not waiting in ambush."

"Likely vagrants," Ephraim observed. He stuck his head into the building again, then withdrew it with a sour expression, "judging by the *smell*."

Liliana nodded, having noticed the stale scent as well.

It seemed Catherine truly was in dire straits if she would stoop to staying in such a place.

"Let's go," she muttered, suddenly feeling guilty for turning Catherine away at all.

Catherine had never done her any favors, nor had she helped Arhyen for that matter, but she *was* his mother. She was his creator, just as Fairfax Breckinridge had been Liliana's. She might have mixed feelings toward her late *father*, but she would always be grateful to him for granting her existence. If she found him in a rundown building amongst other vagrants, she would undoubtedly try to help him . . . although she'd never get that chance since he was dead.

Ephraim followed behind her silently as she inspected the lower floor of the building. Once they'd walked inside the voices upstairs had gone quiet, perhaps worried that an officer of the Watch had come to vacate them. With the nights growing icy cold, such an eviction could possibly mean death.

Not feeling overly worried that any of the building's inhabitants would attack her, she hurried across the open expanse, marred only by a few crates and some scraps of paper and dust, then up a set of steel stairs. She and Ephraim reached the second story to find the scent of smoke heavy in the air, as if lanterns and candles had been blown out upon their appearance. She could see a few forms huddled together on the far side of the room, though she wasn't sure if Ephraim could see them in the limited light.

"Catherine?" she called out, not wanting to worry the building's inhabitants more than necessary. She wasn't there to chase them out.

The figures huddled at the other side of the room muttered softly to each other, then went silent.

Liliana could barely make out the piles of debris around them, but it seemed like they'd amassed quite a few blankets, and had used crates to form partial walls, topped with now-dark lanterns.

"I'm just looking for Catherine," she called again. "If you can point me toward her, I will leave you in peace."

Ephraim stood perfectly still at her side, allowing her to do the talking.

"They took her!" a small voice called out.

There was a hiss of admonishment and a light rasp of impact, like someone swatting someone else.

"Took her where?" she questioned.

She could see a bit of struggle taking place amongst the huddling figures. Ephraim stepped forward, his hand on his pistol, but Liliana reached out and touched his arm to calm him. She presumed that due to the darkness, he feared they might be attacked.

The struggle across the room ended, and a small figure wrapped in a heavy blanket trotted toward them. As it neared, Liliana realized it was a young girl, likely ten or eleven. Her dirty face was framed by a halo of tangled blonde hair, though it was difficult to tell the exact color in the limited light.

"They took her," the girl said again, looking down shyly.

Liliana took a step toward her and knelt down to her level. She'd never really spent any time around children, and was unsure of how to address the young girl, so she'd have to just speak to her like she would any other adult.

"Who took her?" she questioned softly.

The girl glanced over her shoulder to the waiting huddled forms, likely her parents, too cowardly to step forward and protect their daughter from the threat of strangers.

She turned back toward Liliana, then glanced past her toward Ephraim, a wary look in her eyes.

"It's alright," Liliana comforted. "We won't tell anyone you're here."

Turning back to her, the girl nodded. "My mom and brother weren't here when they came, so I hid. I saw them take the old lady. She said her name was Catherine."

"Who were they?" Liliana asked softly.

The little girl shrugged, bunching up the blanket around her shoulders. "They wore uniforms and all looked the same."

Liliana glanced back at Ephraim.

"She could be referring to anyone," he muttered, "officers of the Watch or the Queen's Guard, or mill workers or bakers. They all dress the same as their peers."

"They had fancy hats," the girl chimed in.

Ephraim gazed down at her. "Can you describe these *fancy* hats?"

The girl stepped back, clearly afraid.

"It's okay-" Liliana began, but was cut off as one of the huddled figures hissed, "Nora!"

The little girl looked worried for a second, then hurried back into the darkness where her parents waited. "Leave us be!" the same voice hissed.

"I see they finally gathered their courage," Ephraim commented caustically.

"Should we question them further?" Liliana whispered. That the men's hats were fancy surely narrowed the search, but the girl could probably tell them more.

Ephraim shook his head. "Leave them be. I believe the girl is either talking about the Watch or the Queen's Guard, and given the Guard would have no reason to infiltrate this building to arrest someone like Catherine, it was most likely the Watch."

With one final glance at the huddled figures, Liliana turned back toward the stairs and began to descend. "So where do we go from here?" she questioned softly as Ephraim moved to descend at her side.

"Do we truly need to find this woman?" he asked. "It seems to me she would have been convenient, but now she has become less so. Perhaps our time would be better spent turning our efforts elsewhere."

Liliana bit her lip in thought, nearly stumbling on the final step before reaching the bottom floor. He might be right. They were running out of time, and she didn't even know if Catherine would be able to help them learn anything new. If she had now been arrested by the Watch, questioning her without witnesses might prove difficult, and might very well be a waste of time.

"Perhaps," she agreed with a sigh. "Though it would ease my mind to know she was arrested for something minor, and does not face execution."

"I'll look into it if we survive," he replied, holding open the building's front door. "Honestly though," he continued, stepping out into the dreary light, "I'm not sure why you'd be concerned with her at all."

"She's Arhyen's mother," she replied instantly, scanning the narrow street for signs of danger. Her encounter with Wilfred was fresh on her mind now that she was out in the open, disobeying Hamlet's recommendation.

"*And*?" Ephraim questioned.

Liliana shook her head and started walking as Ephraim let the door swing shut behind them. "What about *your* parents? " she questioned. "Would you care if they were arrested?"

"My parents were both killed in a coal carriage accident," he stated bluntly, scanning the passersby as they reached Market Street.

That didn't exactly answer her question, but given his parent's grim fates, she decided not to press the issue further. "So," she began, tucking a strand of red hair behind her ear. "If we're not going to find Catherine today, where shall we go next?"

Watching any who passed them by like a hawk, Ephraim did not glance down at her as he replied, "We seek out the contacts we interviewed before Arhyen and I were arrested. If one of them knew to attack you to get to Hamlet, others will too."

Liliana frowned as they left the alley and started walking down the busy street. "But won't they just attack both of us?"

"Most likely," he replied, "but we just have to corner one long enough to question them."

Her frown deepened. "It seems wrong to now go after the people who gave us information in confidence."

He snorted. "You said it yourself, they'll likely attack us first. You don't owe them anything."

"Still," she muttered, "I wish there was another way."

He sighed, finally glancing at her. "Empathy for all will get you killed, my dear. You're better off saving it for the few who offer you the courtesy in return."

She went silent after that, walking along with a new prominent thought on her mind. She felt . . . empathy? That surely wasn't something her father had given her. She couldn't help but wonder, did Hamlet somehow feel it too?

An hour and two carriage rides later, Liliana

and Ephraim found themselves near Tailor Street. Not far from the bustling thoroughfare was a less than affluent neighborhood where one of their contacts lived with his family, at least he did when they last spoke to him.

Tailor Street also housed a shop selling masks like Hamlet's, though Liliana found that mystery less important now. After hearing his story of *why* he wore the mask, she didn't need to know anything else about it. Hearing that he'd had acid dripped down his face to eliminate his response to pain was more than enough information.

After disembarking from the carriage, they hadn't walked far before their interest was diverted. A crowd had gathered around the center of the street, blocking carriages and the occasional automobile from traveling further north. Several officers of the Watch worked to hold the crowd back from whatever they were gawking at, but they were sorely outnumbered.

Pulling his fedora further down to shadow his eyes, likely not wanting to be recognized by his fellow officers, Ephraim pushed his way forward through the crowd.

Liliana reached out and clamped her hand around the fabric of his coat, lest she become lost in the chaos.

They neared the center of the crowd, her view blocked by the backs of those taller than her. Finally, she crouched down and peered around Ephraim's waist, then gasped and stumbled backward at what she saw.

Six men, dressed in matching uniforms, lay dead, sprawled across the street.

Taking a deep breath, she crept forward again to take in the scene. Each of the men appeared to have the exact same injury, their chests soaked through with blood.

Other than a few extra spatters, they seemed otherwise un-mutilated.

"The Queen's Guard," Ephraim muttered, leaning down so she'd hear him over the crowd.

The officers were walking the perimeter of the bodies, shouting at the crowd to stay back, but to little avail. No one walked close enough to touch the bodies, but they formed a gawking circle, showing no signs of dispersing.

Ephraim took one final look at the bodies, then dragged Liliana back out of the crowd. Once they were free, he let her go.

A million questions on her mind, she trotted after him toward the shade of a storefront, far from the crowd.

He leaned against the store front's brick wall, then glared outward. "Your beloved friend Hamlet is to blame for this. Is this part of his plan?"

She narrowed her gaze, suddenly feeling defensive. "How can you possibly know that?"

He rolled his eyes. "Their wounds, Liliana. I've seen him kill men that way with that bloody thin sword he carries. He stabs them in the mid to lower back, coming up below the ribs to pierce their hearts. I guarantee you those men all died in the same way, though if you'd like confirmation after the bodies have been examined, I'm sure I can obtain it for you."

Liliana shook her head in disbelief. "If you say they were all killed in that way, I believe you, but you do not know that it was Hamlet."

He glared at her. "I would be truly shocked if it was not. What exactly did he say to you about this grand plan of his?"

She bit her lip, trying to recall exactly what he'd said, then shook her head. "Only that it would happen in three days time, and that it would be big. He said that men need to learn they cannot control fate."

Ephraim shook his head. "That's utterly ridiculous."

"In what way?" she pressed.

"That an automaton could have a lesson to teach the men he was created by," he blurted, then sharply inhaled. "I apologize, that's not what I meant."

She suddenly found herself close to tears. She knew she was inferior to humans in many ways, but to hear it stated so bluntly, especially by someone she considered a friend, stung.

"You know you're different," he continued, the stern line of his mouth conveying his discomfort. "I only meant that Hamlet, as an automaton without emotions or a moral compass, couldn't possibly hope to teach humanity a lesson."

She shook her head, still fighting back her tears. "If that's the case, then I probably shouldn't agree with him then, should I? While I'm grateful for my existence, what gave my father the right to create me? To treat me like a servant? Like some object that should not have thoughts and feelings? Well I *do* have thoughts and feelings, and I'm pretty sure Hamlet does too."

Ephraim blinked at her in shock for several seconds.

She raised a hand to her mouth, suddenly regretting her outburst. A few members of the crowd had pulled back to watch her curiously.

"Let's get out of here," he muttered, placing a hand on her arm to guide her away.

She tugged her arm out of reach. "We still have to question our contact," she stated indignantly.

Ephraim glanced around warily. "Yes, but we can discuss that once we're through making a scene right across the street from a mass murder."

She frowned, still wishing to express her ire at his insensitive comments, but this time when he reached out his hand, she allowed herself to be guided away.

Soon enough, those who'd turned to look at them shifted their focus back to the crime scene. Several more officers wove their way through the carriages and automobiles all at a standstill, herding the crowd away from the bodies.

They walked on in silence for a long while, and Liliana didn't comment when they went past the street that would take them to their contact's dwelling. After hearing of Catherine's arrest, and seeing the men's bodies, she was beginning to think she should have heeded Hamlet's words and stayed back at the apartment.

Something nagged at her though. Had Hamlet wanted her to stay home not to keep her from danger, but to prevent her from seeing his murder victims? That was, if he was even the culprit, and actually cared what she thought of him.

She shook her head. No, she knew on some level he cared what she thought, he'd proven that to be so. That thought alone convinced her that Ephraim's theory was inaccurate. Hamlet wasn't entirely without emotion.

Eventually they left Tailor Street far behind, and Ephraim, looking weary, stopped in front of a small cafe. He glanced down at her wordlessly.

She nodded. Though her limbs were not tired, she could use a break, if only to allow her thoughts to catch up with her.

They went inside and took one of many empty tables. The round surface was just large enough for two cups of tea, and two small plates containing pastries, which they ordered from the proprietor, a young woman with dark hair.

Liliana nudged her strawberry pastry, covered in heavy cream, across her plate. She possessed an unparalleled love for sweets, but found herself unable to enjoy this one.

Ephraim picked at his croissant, but little of it seemed to be reaching his mouth. "Why do you believe Hamlet can feel emotions?" he asked abruptly.

She opened her mouth to speak, then closed it, unsure of how to begin. "I can just tell," she said finally. "If he had no emotions, he would have no motivation for anything he does. If he had no emotions, he would have continued to blindly obey orders. He hates those who created him, and hate is just as much of an emotion as love, or anything else."

Ephraim raised an eyebrow at her and took a sip of his tea. "You're not telling me that he's capable of *love*?"

She shrugged and looked down at her pastry. "Perhaps. Perhaps not. It's not important now. If he *is* responsible for killing those men, he has a good reason. At least, a reason that seems good to him. And we need to figure out what that reason is."

Abandoning his mutilated croissant, Ephraim raised a hand to stroke his chin. "Murdering members of the Queen's Guard to teach mankind a lesson for playing God," he muttered thoughtfully, then lowered his hand to retrieve his teacup, though he did not drink.

Liliana observed him for several seconds.

Finally, he lowered his cup back to the table. "There are only three possible conclusions, as far as I can see," he began, keeping his voice low to avoid being overheard. He held up a finger. "One, the men killed were corrupt, secretly involving themselves either with the LN, or one of the splinter groups, just as Christoph had done." He held up a second finger. "Two, those men *were* members of the LN or aforementioned splinter groups, only *posing* as officers of the Queen's Guard." He held up a third finger. "Three, the entirety of the Queen's Guard, and perhaps the Queen herself, are somehow involved with the scientific experiments Hamlet is protesting. If that is the case, his message is quite clear. Answer his demands, or anyone could be next."

Liliana felt suddenly dizzy. If the third option was true, and the Queen herself was involved with the LN, how on earth was she going to rescue Arhyen? How was she going to rescue *herself*? She'd already been targeted once for her connections with Hamlet. If he intended to teach London a lesson, would she, Arhyen, and Ephraim suffer the consequences?

Hamlet had already murdered six men, leaving their bodies to make a spectacle. If that was only the first step in his plan, what would be the finale?

CHAPTER 6

Arhyen drummed his fingers anxiously across his knee, then reached up to straighten his charcoal waistcoat over his predominantly white pinstriped shirt. His tan trouser-clad legs dangled over the edge of his rickety bed. Though he was pleased to be back in regular clothes, he would have preferred something more . . . black. He also would have preferred Wakefield be on time for their meeting.

Not that he knew what time it was.

Still, he'd been told *morning*, and judging by the rumble in his stomach, it was well toward noon. While waiting, he'd reviewed his file a few more times, but struggled to make full sense of it. Even most of what the London Network had done to save him was difficult to grasp. He was quite sure he'd never heard of the medicines used to stave off his infections, and to prevent his body from killing off the foreign, synthetic organs placed within him.

The confusing pages also begged the question of *why*? He'd asked for leverage, some sort of information that should it get out, would be disastrous for the London Network. Were the details of what was done to him supposed to suffice?

He jumped as the lock clunked in the nearby door. The door swung inward, admitting Wakefield and his usual two-person entourage. Wakefield's skin was flushed, and his normally perfectly groomed gray hair was mussed. Something was wrong.

"Forgive me the delay," Wakefield announced. "That monster has struck again. Six of my men now lay dead in the street."

Arhyen gave him a deadpan expression. If Wakefield had intended to surprise him, he'd have to do a lot better than that.

Wakefield marched toward Arhyen's bedside, then waited as his chair was moved to the back of his knees. Without looking to ensure it was positioned correctly, he sat. "You don't seem surprised about this mass murder," he commented, eyeing Arhyen up and down.

Arhyen arched an eyebrow at him. "Are you implying I somehow had something to do with it?"

Wakefield scoffed. "Hardly. I have faith in the security of this compound. I'm simply commenting on the fact that you do not seem surprised Hamlet would murder six officers of the Queen's Guard."

He shrugged. "I know of his capabilities."

"And yet you would give us conditions while we're running out of time?" Wakefield countered.

He smirked. "I'm not protecting him, if that's what you mean. I am simply protecting myself. While I'm well aware of Hamlet's aptitude for violence, I also know the London Network. You can play the role of good guy all you please, you're not fooling anyone."

The flush on Wakefield's lined cheeks grew brighter.

He began taking deep breaths, as if to calm his temper. Failing, he slammed his palm against the arm of his chair, then jumped to his feet.

"Fine!" he snapped. "We believe our dead men are only the beginning. Hamlet is planning something big, and must be stopped. If you can help us find him, we will meet any and every demand you have."

Arhyen stood and held out his hand. "I want only to guarantee my safety, and that of my associates, nothing more."

Wakefield took his hand and gave it a rough shake. "A wise choice." He pulled his hand away, then resumed his seat.

Arhyen chose to remain standing, slightly wary of Wakefield's temper. He'd rather be on his feet when he got a chair thrown at him.

"I see you've been reading your file," Wakefield commented, gesturing to the dog-eared pile of papers on his bedside table. "This is the information you need for leverage."

He glanced at the papers, then back to Wakefield. "How so?"

Wakefield sighed. "You are living proof that we have the technology to cure most any illness. We can replace failing organs, and we can care for the body well enough that one might survive the process. This was the missing piece the group who worked on you had not accounted for." He reached into his coat pocket, then withdrew a small vial of vibrant blue liquid. "*This* is what saved your life."

Arhyen peered at the vial, wondering if it was simply a nice hue of ink and Wakefield was bluffing. "Even if what you say is true, I don't see how it will provide me with leverage."

Wakefield returned the vial to his pocket. "The London Network has the power to cure most any illness. Even illnesses of the blood or constitution. This formula," he patted the pocket where he'd placed the vial, "causes the body to enter a rapid state of healing. If you were to drink this entire vial at once, you could cut yourself, and it would heal within minutes. You would have died without this treatment."

He scowled. "If it could heal a cut almost instantly, why are my incisions still uncomfortable?"

Wakefield looked him up and down. "You were near death when you were brought to us. Rapid healing of that magnitude can do its own damage to the body. You could have gone into shock." He cleared his throat. "The cure is also expensive and time consuming to manufacture."

Arhyen snorted. If he had to guess, he'd say the London Network had been less concerned about shock, and more concerned about wasting their precious cure on a lowly thief.

"So it can *cure* any illness?" he reiterated, still unable to believe Wakefield's claims.

He shrugged. "I suppose cure is not the right word. It can heal the damage done by any illness. The illness itself may still remain, but if the victim continued to take this medicine to heal themselves, they could survive until old age eventually took them. With this," he patted his pocket again, "thousands of lives could be saved. Yet, we keep it hidden because it is difficult and expensive to produce."

Arhyen's eyes widened as he realized what Wakefield was trying to say. "The Queen knows of this miraculous cure, and she's keeping it hidden while her loyal subjects die their natural, and sometimes unnatural deaths, just to avoid arousing suspicion. If the people of London were to find out that such information has been kept for them, while they lose their loved ones to consumption and pneumonia, they would rebel. It would be chaos."

Wakefield nodded. "Precisely. I will provide you with several vials of this substance, along with copies of your medical records. You will be released to deliver them to whomever you see fit, then you will either return to us immediately with information on Hamlet's whereabouts, or you will stop him yourself. Fail to do so, and we will hunt you down, along with any person who has so much as muttered your name in the span of their entire lives."

He stroked his stubbly chin in thought. Was it worth it? If he failed to locate Hamlet, it could result in the LN discovering Liliana. Yet if he did not try, they might do so anyway. At least if he *did* manage to turn over Hamlet, there was a slim chance they would be safe. He had no idea who he'd give the vials to for leverage, but the LN didn't know that. It was as good a plan as he was going to get.

He gestured toward the door. "Shall we? If I have a time limit, I'd like to get started right away."

Not as seemingly pleased as he should have been after making the deal he wanted, Wakefield stood. He gestured to his two men to lead the way to the door.

Arhyen couldn't quite believe it. He was getting out. He'd actually managed to talk his way out of what could have easily been the end of his life.

Now he just had to somehow help the London Network take down a murderous automaton who'd been created as a weapon. An automaton capable of killing men in seconds. An automaton who might very well be at Liliana's side that very moment.

Arhyen shivered as he followed Wakefield out of the room. Perhaps his life would end quite soon after all, if not at the hands of the LN, then at the end of Hamlet's sword.

❧

LILIANA PEERED ACROSS THE STREET AT WATCH Headquarters, wishing desperately for some sort of disguise. While no one else had attacked her, she felt vulnerable waiting in plain view for such an extended period of time.

Ephraim had gone inside roughly twenty minutes ago. After discussing the possibilities while they rested at the cafe, they'd come to the conclusion that they should confirm the murdered men as officers of the Queen's Guard before they started exploring the various scenarios. If they were simply imposters, then perhaps Hamlet was just targeting members of the LN or splinter groups, and the Queen had nothing to do with it. If the entire city government was involved with the LN, she feared she and Arhyen would have to flee the city after she rescued him, though she wasn't sure he'd agree to leave. He had a stubborn streak, just like Ephraim, and . . . well, just like herself.

Pushing away from the brick wall, she inched toward a nearby alcove, hoping to at least shield herself partially from sight. Her boots skidded across the icy muck leftover from the storm, taking most of her concentration. She was almost to the alcove when a woman's scream cut through the air.

She tensed, listening intently for another scream. Instead of one, she heard many, along with frantic shouts. The scent of smoke hit her nostrils.

Glancing at Watch Headquarters, she debated her options. She and Ephraim had limited time to unravel

Hamlet's mystery, but what if this was Hamlet's next move? Surely Ephraim would know just where she went if he emerged to find her missing.

She was about to take off toward the sound of the shouts when Ephraim, along with three officers in uniform, burst forth from the double doors of their building. Her eyes met Ephraim's for a split second, acknowledging his unsaid message. As he jogged down one side of the street, she took off down the other, opposite him.

Soon enough, she caught sight of smoke, more hazy gray than the black coal smoke common in the city. Judging by the amount spewing upward to meld with the dreary sky, the fire was large enough to encompass several buildings.

She slowed as she reached the gathering crowd, and the fire that had drawn them. She gazed up at the bright orange flames licking the sky.

"There were people inside!" a woman gasped somewhere to her left.

"The fire spread too quickly," another muttered.

She strained her hearing to pick out any other comments.

"This is only the beginning," she heard someone whisper amongst the murmur of the crowd.

"They'll pay for what they've done to us," another whispered back.

Liliana hopped on her toes, attempting to see who she'd overheard, but the crowd was tightly packed and milling around. It was impossible to tell.

"By jove, you run fast," a voice panted behind her.

She turned to see Ephraim, hunched over with a pale sheen of sweat on his face. She blushed, realizing she'd run faster than any human should. She could only hope everyone had been too distracted by the fire to notice, lest they question why an automaton was out on her own.

Glancing around warily, she whispered, "I heard someone talking about the fire. It sounded like they knew something about why it was started. Whoever they were speaking to said, *They'll pay for what they've done*."

Ephraim gazed up past the crowd at the burning building. Efforts were now being made to put out the fire, but it seemed like a lost cause. The officers who'd accompanied Ephraim were now pushing back the crowd, and Liliana had to step back to avoid being trampled. Not readily identifiable as an officer, Ephraim received the same treatment.

He grabbed her arm and guided her further away. "You do realize what that building was, do you not?"

Trotting beside him, she shook her head.

Once they were well out of reach of the crowd, he stopped and released her. "It was an office of the Royal Society."

"Royal Society?" she questioned, unfamiliar with the organization.

"A society of science-minded individuals," he explained, keeping his voice low. "Fairfax Breckinridge and Victor Ashdown were both members."

"How do you know that?" she gasped as the pieces fell into place.

"I did my research when you first came to London," he explained nonchalantly.

She frowned. "Research regarding me? You didn't trust me to tell the truth?"

He smirked. "Foolish girl, you assume just because you bat your big innocent eyes that all should trust you immediately? I had only just met you when I had to sneak you into London without papers."

Her frown deepened as they began to walk further away from the fire. "Back to this Royal Society. What do they do?"

He shrugged. "What does any scientific or philosophical organization do? Sit around and talk about their ideas so they can pretend they're somehow wiser than everyone else. While some alchemists and physicians may be worthwhile, the actual organization is pointless."

"So why target their building?" she questioned. "What would Hamlet have to gain?"

"Well I'd say he obviously wanted to kill whoever was inside," he replied. "I've confirmed that the dead men who were left on Tailor Street were officers of the Queen's guard, all well established. They were not a unit, and likely would not have been caught together, so it's safe to assume they were targeted one by one, then their bodies were placed post-mortem. I could not find any record of Catherine's arrest either, by the way, so it must have been the Guard who took her."

He glanced over his shoulder toward the burning building again, then forward as he continued walking. "Now we'll have more dead men to identify, though it will be difficult with the fire. We'll likely have to wait until their families report them missing."

She chewed her lip, digesting the information. "So we know that Hamlet is targeting each of these men for a reason, but we do not know what that reason is, nor who will be next. We have no way of stopping him, or knowing if he should even be stopped."

"Of course he should be stopped," Ephraim snapped.

They reached the end of Market Street and continued in the direction of Arhyen's apartment.

Liliana took a deep breath. "I'm not entirely sure he

should be stopped. Are we not against the London Network?"

Ephraim shrugged, keeping his eyes forward. "Who knows? As far as I'm concerned, we may have been dealing with only the splinter groups this entire time. We have no idea the intent of the actual organization, especially if the Queen's Guard is somehow involved."

Liliana shook her head. "I believe they killed my father, and I believe that they create automatons only to torture them and force them to obey, and now they're holding Arhyen prisoner because they want to find Hamlet and torture or kill him. I cannot in good conscience think of them as anything but my enemies."

Ephraim was silent for several seconds as their footfalls echoed off the buildings surrounding the narrow street they'd entered. Finally, he shook his head. "For a frighteningly intelligent woman, you are frustratingly naive."

She scowled over at him. "I am not."

He shook his head again. "Ninety percent of the information we've obtained has been from Hamlet. Only a fool would blindly believe all they're told from a single source. For all you know *he* killed your father."

"He did *not*," she snapped, unsure of why she was arguing so vehemently. She couldn't be wrong about *everything*.

"No?" he pressed. "You've seen how quickly and silently he can kill. You have incredibly perceptive senses, yet you never saw your father's killer, nor did you hear any struggle. You simply found him, *dead*."

She stopped walking and turned toward him. "How do you know that?" she gasped.

He had the grace to look slightly abashed. "Arhyen told me the details," he admitted, "and I've believed

Hamlet the culprit since we first laid eyes upon him. He was ready for you as soon as you entered the city. I believe he followed you here, all the way from your father's compound."

"My father died a long time before Arhyen found me," she argued. "Are you suggesting Hamlet waited in the woods all that time?"

"No," he replied thoughtfully. "He committed crimes within the city during that time frame so he could not have been waiting out there all along. *But* he already admitted he knew Arhyen had been hired to find your father's journal beforehand. I think it likely he followed him to the compound, then followed the both of you back."

She shook her head over and over. He had to be wrong. He was jumping to so many conclusions without a shred of proof. Anyone could have killed her father.

"My, what an excellent detective," a voice commented from above.

Liliana whipped her gaze around the empty street, then finally settled on the roof of a nearby building. Atop the low roof sat Hamlet in his customary mask and low top hat.

"Thank you," Ephraim said cooly. "I *know*."

Hamlet inclined his head, then hopped down from the top of the building, barely making a sound as his feet touched down.

"Y-you're not saying he's right?" Liliana stammered, completely caught off guard. How long had he been listening to them?

He nodded, not making a move to close the distance between them. "I apologize for misleading you, but I did not want you to judge me for my actions. Unfortunately, it is all as he said. I followed Mr. Croft to your father's compound, then stowed away on the train you boarded on the way back. This was a long while after I killed Fairfax Breckinridge and failed to find his journal. I had not expected someone like *you* to be there. I fled before my mission was complete."

"B-but why?" she asked, her voice cracking with the bitter sense of betrayal.

"All part of my plan, I'm afraid," he explained. "I apologize for leaving you in the dark for so long, but do not fear, it will be over soon."

Ephraim stepped protectively in front of Liliana, his hand on his pistol.

Hamlet didn't move. "Surely you realize you are not my enemies?"

"Nor are we your friends," Ephraim hissed.

Hot tears betrayed her as she stepped around Ephraim to face Hamlet without fear. "If that is the case, then tell me what all of this is for. Tell me why you murdered my father, and why you followed me to London, if that is truly the case." She took another step toward him, daring him to attack, or to run away.

He didn't move, except to tilt his head. "I'm starting a revolution, my dear, surely you've figured that out by now? Why should these men of science hold all the power? I've never seen an ounce of humanity in any of them. No, I'm going to expose their secrets. They're all frightened now of what I'll do next."

"What about Arhyen!" she cried, finally losing her composure. "What happens to him when your revolution begins!"

"I assure you, he will be safely returned to your side," he replied. "Although, scientific abominations that you both now are, I would not advise remaining within the city."

She glowered at him. “I’m going after Arhyen *now*. You have proven yourself a liar. I no longer trust you to return him to me.”

Hamlet chuckled. “That will not be necessary. I only came to warn you. It seems he has switched sides.”

Liliana was momentarily confused, until she spotted a lone figure at the end of the street. Her heart seemed to skip a beat, then she propelled herself forward. Her feet barely touched the ground as she ran. Moments later, she slammed into Arhyen’s waiting arms. Arhyen. He was somehow free, cradling her in his embrace. Was she dreaming?

He lifted her and spun her around, then gently let her back down to the ground.

Laughing and crying, she pulled away enough to see his face. “How?” she questioned, still not believing her eyes.

“I managed to strike a deal,” he explained, “though we are far from safe. I debated even coming to see you for fear the LN would use you against me, but I couldn’t risk you getting caught up in the perils to come. I need you to leave the city immediately.”

She shook her head, suddenly stunned, and pulled the rest of the way out of his embrace. He seemed thinner than he’d been before, though he appeared well-rested and clean shaven. “W-what?” she stammered. “You have to be joking.”

“I’m entirely serious,” he continued. “If I fail my part of the bargain, they *will* learn of your existence, and they *will* come after you.”

“If they’re still alive,” Ephraim commented, his footsteps signaling his approach to Liliana’s back. “Hamlet might just kill them all.”

Remembering Hamlet, Liliana whipped her gaze over her shoulder, but he was nowhere to be seen.

"One of his famous exits," Ephraim explained. "*And*, I'll do the gentlemanly thing and not say *I told you so*."

She wasn't sure if she wanted to hug him, punch him, or both, and she was having much the same feelings toward Arhyen, though she was still overjoyed to see him alive and well.

Not seeming to notice her conflict, Ephraim turned his questioning gaze to Arhyen. "Now what's this I hear about you switching sides?"

CHAPTER 7

"What did they do to you?" Liliana questioned as they walked back toward the apartment. Before Arhyen could answer, she continued, "You said you struck a deal to get out. What kind of deal? Are you going to be alright? Do you need to sit down and take a break?"

Ephraim remained silent as he walked by her other side, not offering Arhyen the least bit of assistance.

Arhyen stopped walking. Facing her, he forced a smile, masking his agitation at seeing Hamlet with her. "I assure you, I'm fine, and I will explain everything as soon as we get back to the apartment." He began to walk, then stopped again. Though he wanted to wait until they were safe within the apartment to explain things, *his* question simply couldn't wait.

"What was Hamlet doing here?" he blurted. "Do you know where he's going?" Perhaps if she already knew Hamlet's plan, he could tell Wakefield and get them out of this entire mess.

She frowned. "No, we just know that he," she hesitated, glanced at Ephraim, then shook her head, "it doesn't matter."

He wanted to press the issue, but her expression stopped him. He reached up and wiped a single tear as it slid down her cheek.

"Would you care to tell us what on earth is going on?" Ephraim interrupted, stepping up behind him.

He sighed and lowered his hand. "We'll need to stop by the apartment. I'll explain everything there, then we'll leave for the train station." He felt instant pain at the notion, yet, he *had* to do it. He had to let her go if he wanted to save her from the London Network, and from whatever Hamlet was planning.

Liliana's hurt expression quickly turned hostile. She stomped her foot. "I'm *not* going. I'm more physically capable of surviving than *you* are. If anyone is to stay, it should be me."

He shook his head, then gently took her arm to keep her walking. She might be more physically capable, but she might not be for long. He briefly debated telling her about the changes to his blood composition, but quickly dismissed the idea. She had enough to worry about. He wanted her focused on her own survival.

"I'm not going," she muttered again as they walked.

He remained silent until they reached the apartment. Truth be told, he didn't feel the need to rest at all. Physically, he felt magnificent. Was it all thanks to the bright blue liquid, contained within several vials in his front pocket? Did it matter?

He waited while Liliana unlocked the apartment, then opened the door. She went in first, followed by Arhyen, then Ephraim, who shut and locked the door behind him.

Arhyen gazed around his apartment. *Their* apartment,

really, for it surely belonged to Liliana as much as it did to him at this point...though it might not belong to either of them if they didn't pay rent soon.

It was all well enough, they might not need it by tomorrow.

He moved forward and stepped around the sofa, peering curiously at the mess on the low table. He recognized the largest device as a microscope, though he'd never used one. There were a few books, a few empty beakers, a pair of long tweezers, and various scattered papers. He leaned over, eyeing the papers more closely.

He lifted one in his hand, then turned back to Ephraim and Liliana, who were both watching him expectantly. "What is this?" he questioned, gesturing at the stained paper in his hand.

Liliana stepped forward. "We're not sure. It was found in the Watch Captain's home."

He looked down at the paper again. The Captain of the Watch had been involved with one of the splinter groups of the LN. It couldn't be a coincidence. With his free hand, he lifted one of the vials from his pocket, then held it next to the largest stain on the paper.

Liliana hurried to his side, her gaze affixed to the vial. "Where did you get that?" she gasped.

He glanced over to meet her gaze. "This is my leverage against the LN. It's a medicine."

She looked up at him in shock, then shook her head. "This," she pointed to the stained paper, "was found all over the Captain's home. It was still fresh when he was arrested, so it likely happened the night before his confession."

He pursed his lips in thought. They really shouldn't be hanging around talking about this. They needed to get moving . . . but, "Perhaps he was given a cure to his illness in exchange for confessing his crimes?"

Ephraim joined them, snatching the vial from Arhyen's hand. He glared down at it in his palm. "Christoph, the former Captain of the Watch, is dead. He was found in his cell with no signs of foul play. If this was the *cure* given to him, it did not work."

Arhyen's eyes widened. "Well I sincerely hope we are mistaken, because this was the same cure given to *me*."

While Liliana appeared horrified, Ephraim just seemed thoughtful. "In what way do these vials serve as leverage?" he asked.

"This may come as quite a shock," Arhyen began, "but in order to explain that, I must explain something else first. The London Network is not an independent, underground organization, as we once thought. They are actually in the employ of the Queen, or so I've been told. I have no actual proof, but I believe the man who provided me with this information to be genuine."

"Oh," Ephraim began, sarcasm clear in his tone. "So *that* must be why six verified members of the Queen's Guard were killed, and why an office of the Royal Society was set aflame."

His meeting with Wakefield flitted through his mind, recalling his rage at losing his men. "Then he *was* telling me the truth," he mused. "He told me his men had been attacked by Hamlet."

"Along with Liliana's father," Ephraim added.

Arhyen turned in time to see her scowl at Ephraim, but her expression softened as it turned toward him. He'd been longing to feel her gaze every single moment of the past weeks. He soaked it in, knowing he'd likely not have it again after today. He could not risk it. He should not be enjoying it now at all.

Seeming to think he was gazing at her in hopes of an explanation, she began, "Yes, he not only killed my father, but followed you to my father's compound, knowing you were searching for his journal, which he had failed to obtain."

Arhyen's gut clenched, remembering the brief glimpse of the masked figure he'd seen in the woods outside of the compound. "How could he have failed?" he asked. "All I had to do was ask you for it."

Her brow furrowed in confusion as she shook her head. "He said he did not expect me to be there, so he fled."

"But he had already killed your father," Ephraim added. "Why not kill you as well?"

"Because she's somehow part of his plan," Arhyen decided.

He'd already thought Hamlet unhealthily concerned with Liliana, and now there was just too much proof to deny it any longer. His mind flashed again to the masked figure watching them in the woods.

"He left her alive," Arhyen explained, "then followed me on my journey to retrieve the journal. He followed me all the way to the compound, yet, he did not steal the journal until we were back in the city. If he was only concerned with that, he could have taken it right away. Instead, he waited until Liliana was in London." He turned toward her. "This is all the more reason for you to leave the city. He wanted you to be here."

She met his gaze defiantly. "It's all the more reason for me to confront Hamlet once more and finally learn just why my father had to die. Why so many others have died. *And*," she pointed to the vial still in Ephraim's grasp, "I will learn just what *that* is, and why it killed

Christoph. I will not let the same fate befall you." She aimed her unyielding gaze at Arhyen.

He swallowed the lump in his throat. Had this been the LN's plan all along? Make him well long enough to be of use, then let their concoction kill him, tying up all loose ends?

He turned to Ephraim. "That vial, along with two others, is my main source of leverage. I claimed I would distribute them to trustworthy contacts, who would then demonstrate the serum to the public, should I be killed. As I need to get Liliana out of the city, I must leave that task to you."

Ephraim crossed his arms. At first Arhyen thought he might deny his request, then he smirked. "I'll do as you ask, but first I'd like to watch your attempt at convincing *her* to leave. I suspect it will be quite entertaining."

"Yes, *quite* entertaining," Liliana echoed stubbornly.

Arhyen slumped onto the sofa with a groan. "You don't seem to understand. I've risked them finding you in coming here. The actual London Network did not know of this apartment, or much about any of us, but now surely I was followed. I came here now, because I could not risk them finding this place later, with you still around." He turned his gaze up to her. "You must leave today. There is no other choice."

Tears began to stream down her face. She peered down at him, utterly betrayed.

"I'll give you two a moment," Ephraim muttered, then made his way toward the door. With a few soft clicks, he let himself outside.

Once they were alone, Liliana's tears flowed more heavily.

He sighed. "Liliana, I-"

"How *dare* you," she hissed, interrupting him. "I have

been waiting here for weeks, not knowing if you were alive or dead. When I tried to rescue you, Hamlet claimed I would only put you in danger. I have been utterly helpless. I swore to myself when I first came to London that I would never feel as helpless as I did when I was with my father, yet here I was."

"Liliana, I was only trying to-" he began, trying to calm her, but she persisted.

"No," she snapped. "I don't want to hear about what you were trying to do. You should have swept me off my feet with a kiss. Then you should have asked me how I've been. Then we should have formulated a plan together, utilizing both our strengths, and supplementing for each other's weaknesses. *That's* how a partnership works."

He was utterly dumbfounded. She truly wanted him to sweep her off her feet with a kiss? He would have gladly obliged had he known he was allowed, and had he not been solely focused on the idea of keeping her alive.

She was glaring at him, red faced, panting after her outburst.

He did the only thing he could think to do. He stood, wrapped his arms around her, then swept her off her feet with a kiss.

LILIANA'S HEART THREATENED TO ESCAPE HER THROAT. Though she'd wanted Arhyen to kiss her, she hadn't expected him to right then and there. The stubble on his chin tickled her face, reminding her that he'd spent the past weeks in captivity. She suddenly felt a bit guilty for her outburst. At least she'd been free.

She wrapped her arms tightly around his waist as he slowly pulled his mouth away from hers. She didn't actually regret expressing her anger one bit since it had gotten her what she wanted, but really, he didn't deserve it. She had no idea what he'd been through.

A knock preceded Ephraim's re-entry. Startled, Liliana pulled away and hopped back several paces, blushing furiously.

Ephraim watched her with a raised brow as he shut the door behind him. "If you two are quite through, I believe London will soon be in utter chaos, and we should probably do something."

"What?" she and Arhyen blurted in unison.

"I walked down the street to the intersection and witnessed a few people running past," he explained. "More buildings have caught fire with people inside them, and there are rumors that London Bridge has suffered explosion damage."

Liliana chewed her lip in thought. Would these be isolated incidents like the others, or was London really about to go up in flames?

"I was supposed to have more time than this," Arhyen groaned. "I was supposed to help the LN locate Hamlet before it was too late."

"I'd wager he's still working his way up to his finale," Ephraim suggested. "There may still be time."

"To turn him in?" Liliana interrupted, not thinking before she spoke.

Would she argue such a plan? Hamlet had admitted to killing her father after all, but he'd also saved her life on multiple occasions, and now he'd saved Arhyen's life twice, no, wait, *three times*, she internally corrected, thinking back to the tale of Arhyen and Ephraim nearly dying in a smelter. He may have lied to her, but could she betray him now after all he'd done?

Clearly reading her hesitation, Arhyen approached

and gently took her hands in his. "He has killed countless people," he said softly, "and now he is killing indiscriminately, just to prove a point. Regardless of how we feel about the London Network, Hamlet must be stopped, and in stopping him, there is the chance that we may finally be safe."

She chewed her lip hard enough to nearly draw blood. She knew he was right, but it just didn't *feel* right. The sick feeling in her gut told her this was not a decision she should be making.

"Let us find him," she breathed. "Perhaps he can be convinced to stop what he's doing."

Arhyen nodded, then pulled away. "Perhaps," he sighed, then reached into the same pocket from which he'd withdrawn the blue-filled vial, only this time, he produced a black-filled one. He handed it to her. "If we cannot reason with him, we only need to convince him to drink this. It will cause his nervous system to shut down long enough for him to be destroyed."

Barely breathing, she stared down at the vial in her hand. "I thought you said we were turning him in."

"Yes," he replied. "Dead or alive. When it comes to Hamlet, we all know the only real option."

She wrapped her fingers around the small vial, then buried her hands in the folds of her skirt to hide their trembling. She knew why Arhyen had handed her the vial. If anyone could convince Hamlet to drink, it was her. The only question was, could she do it? Could she avenge her father's death by killing Hamlet?

She supposed the more appropriate question was, did she *want* to?

CHAPTER 8

The vial of poison felt heavy in Liliana's coat pocket. She watched as Arhyen moved around the apartment, preparing himself for the trials to come. Ephraim remained with them, not wanting to risk returning to Watch Headquarters, only to lose track of her and Arhyen in the chaos. They'd placed one vial of the blue liquid into a small safe hidden under a tile in the bathroom, and Ephraim and Liliana each took one of the remaining two. Should the LN later come after any of them, they knew what to do, but that was a worry for a later time.

Liliana straightened her black coat over her trousers and shirt for the hundredth time. Though it was straight to begin with, she just couldn't help her nerves. Her garb would make her stand out amongst other women, but with buildings burning and people dying, no one would notice her clothing.

Completely lost in her thoughts, she startled as Arhyen approached and placed his hands on her shoulders.

She blinked up at him.

"Are you sure you want to be a part of this?" he asked softly, worry creasing his brow. "It's not too late to get you out of the city, and you know that would be my preference."

She took a shaky breath. *Did* she want to be a part of this? She wanted to help Arhyen and Ephraim, and to keep them both safe. She didn't want any other innocent people dying. But did she want to side with the London Network? Did she want to murder Hamlet? Did she owe it to her father to avenge him?

"I'm not leaving the city," she answered finally. She'd have to find the other answers soon enough, but for now, that was what she knew for sure. She would not be leaving the city, not unless Arhyen came with her, and he seemed dead set on seeing his mission through to the end.

His shoulders slumped in defeat, but he nodded, accepting her answer. "If I can't make you run away to safety, I need you to at least make me a promise."

She hesitated, wondering what he might ask, then nodded for him to go on.

He took a deep breath, peering straight into her eyes. "Promise me that should I no longer be around, you won't let Hamlet drag you down with him. That is my only dying wish."

"Dying wish!" she gasped, tugging against his grip on her shoulders, but he refused to let go. Ceasing her half-hearted struggles, she muttered, "You're *not* going to die."

"My dear," he began patiently, removing one hand from her shoulder to lift her chin with his finger. "Things aren't looking good for any of us, but especially not for me. If what you've told me about the Captain of the Watch is true, I may not have much time left. This so called cure to my ailments may only be temporary. So please, just promise me."

"I promise," she grumbled, "but you're not going to die. I won't allow it."

He smiled. "Thank you, now we should get moving before there's no city left to save."

He withdrew his hands and stepped back. They simultaneously turned to Ephraim who'd been standing near the sofa quietly observing them.

He patted his waistcoat pocket where he'd hidden his vial of blue liquid. His pistol was strapped at his side, only visible in brief glances whenever his long charcoal coat shifted out of the way. His customary fedora shaded his pale eyes, which sparkled with excitement.

"We'll head to Market Street first," Arhyen announced. "I don't know what's going on out there, but if Hamlet is causing all of this, someone must have seen him."

Liliana nodded, not sure if she agreed. Hamlet was adept at not being seen. Yet, it was still as good a plan as any, and she suspected if Hamlet saw her, he might reveal himself and save them the search. He wanted to keep her alive, at least for now. She wasn't sure why, especially since he'd just admitted to killing her father.

Arhyen placed his hand on her shoulder to regain her attention. "Are you ready?"

She looked up at him and nodded, still thinking about the possibility of Hamlet revealing himself. He'd likely only do so if she were alone. If she could manage that, then perhaps she could convince him to halt his revolution. She found she really didn't want to kill him.

Of course, he might be too busy wreaking havoc to notice her, then she'd be all alone in the chaotic city, filled with people doing their best to not get burned alive.

Ephraim moved past her to open the door.

Hand in hand, she and Arhyen followed him. One way or another, everything would soon be over. She would have liked to think there was a chance she and Arhyen could survive to live a normal life together, but there was little hope of that. Either Arhyen would die like the Captain of the Watch had, or she would eventually go mad like Hamlet. The third option, was they would both soon be killed in the chaos. Perhaps that was a preferable fate to the alternatives.

Just like in her adventure novels, when the outlook was grim, the very least one could do was go out in a blaze of glory. Of course, the heroes usually still lived, and the villains died. If she wasn't willing to kill the villain, would she die like one herself?

❧

THE SCENT OF SMOKE BURNED ARHYEN'S LUNGS AS soon as they exited the apartment. Screams and cries could be heard in the distance. He reluctantly released Liliana's hand, wishing with all his heart he'd tried harder to convince her to leave. Truth was, he wanted her by his side. He could hardly bear the thought of putting her on a train, knowing he might never see her again.

It was too late now either way. He doubted the trains were still running, and the closest city gates were likely already clogged with people trying to escape Hamlet's terrorism.

Ephraim led the way down the narrow street toward the first intersection, his long coat flapping in the icy wind.

Arhyen tried to keep his eyes on their surroundings, but it was difficult to keep his gaze off Liliana. She stalked along silently, like a tiny predator, dressed all in black with her hair tucked up beneath her cap. If anything happened to her . . .

He shook his head, then watched as Ephraim peered both ways down the intersection. Suddenly he stepped back, and a woman with several children ran by, heading in the opposite direction of Market Street. Once they'd passed, Ephraim peered down the street again, then signaled that all was clear.

With Liliana at his side, Arhyen jogged to catch up to Ephraim. They continued on that way until they reached Market Street, the source of the horrible screams. Not only screams, though. Maniacal laughter could be heard in short bursts, along with angry shouting. The chill wind had picked up, carrying the screams and shouts at varying volumes through the air. Flakes of ice stung Arhyen's skin, distracting him. He wrapped his coat more tightly around himself with one arm, and placed a hand on his cap with the other.

"What in the blazes is going on?" Ephraim muttered, peeking out toward the main street as he shielded his face from the flurries of ice.

They were on the edge of the district, a block before the storefronts began, but it was close enough to see what was happening. *Too close*, Arhyen thought as a blood splattered man stumbled into their alleyway.

He reached out his arm and pushed Liliana out of the man's path. The man staggered on, muttering to himself as if he'd gone mad. A moment later, a laughing woman ran past them, continuing down the main street.

A sick knot was growing in Arhyen's stomach. These

people weren't just victims of fire and violence. They'd been affected by something *else*.

He turned his gaze toward Liliana, meeting her wide eyes. "Do you think . . . " he trailed off.

She nodded, then whispered, "My father's synthetic emotions. We knew this was a possibility. Hamlet must have used them to drive everyone mad." She pushed wayward strands of her red hair back from her face as another man, sobbing and wiping tears from his eyes, stumbled past their hiding spot.

"Is it permanent?" Ephraim hissed, glancing back at them, before quickly returning his gaze to the street.

"I don't think so," she explained to his back. "I questioned Hamlet once about the emotions my father administered to me. He seemed to believe they had long since worn off. My brain developed my current emotions using the instinctual data given to me."

Arhyen frowned. He thought it was a lot more than that. After all, you could not *create* love and hate, and he was quite sure Liliana was capable of both emotions. Although, now was not the time to argue.

"Well there's nothing we can do for these people now," he said instead. "Let's try to find someone coherent enough to tell us if they've seen Hamlet, and if so, which way he went."

Ephraim turned his gaze away from the street, then nodded. "Let us retreat to the side streets. I don't relish the idea of running into anyone infected with rage. Let's find one of the crying ones instead."

LILIANA WAS GLAD TO LEAVE THE MAIN STREET BEHIND.

She seemed to be in a state of shock. Had her father's creation truly caused so much chaos? She knew Hamlet had the formulae for anger, sadness, happiness, and something that felt like love, but wasn't. She supposed she'd call it affection. Had Hamlet manufactured enough of each formulae to infect everyone running around the streets? If so, how had he administered them? It didn't seem to be airborne, since she felt no lingering effects. Perhaps he put it in their food and drink? That would make more sense with the numerous cafes and restaurants on Market Street.

She chewed on her lip as they crept back down the alley, away from the main thoroughfare. With nods of agreement, they took their first left. She expected that at any moment, someone infected with rage would jump out and try to murder them, which made her realize another odd thing. These emotions seemed much more potent than what her father had created. Those infected with happiness should have felt pleasant emotions, but from what they'd seen, they cackled maniacally, on the verge of hysteria. Perhaps interacting with that sort might prove just as bad, if not worse, than a rage infected person.

The first woman they came upon in the alleyway was screaming hysterically, oblivious to their presence. Liliana couldn't even determine which emotion had afflicted her. Could it be more than one? Deeming the woman a lost cause, they moved past her.

The next person they found was an older woman in an expensive, frilly dress, sitting right in a puddle of muck leftover from the snow, crying her eyes out.

Ephraim looked down at her dispassionately. "Pardon us, ma'am, could we ask you a few questions?"

Rubbing her red-rimmed eyes, she peered up at them

for a few seconds, then broke down into another fit of crying.

"It's no use speaking to any of them," Ephraim muttered. "We're wasting time."

"The masked men!" the woman wailed. "T-they made me so, *hiccup*, sad!"

"Masked *men*?" Ephraim inquired curiously. "As in, more than one?"

The woman continued to sob, but did not reply.

He turned to Liliana. "Do you have any knowledge of possible accomplices in this scheme?"

Wide-eyed, she shrugged. She knew Hamlet employed many spies, and it would stand to reason that they could be part of his plan, but she'd never met any of them. This at least ruled out her theory of infected food. This woman appeared to have been accosted directly. The Advector Serum that could be used to administer the emotions was a vapor. Perhaps Hamlet and his associates were spraying it directly into people's faces.

She turned to meet Arhyen's gaze, which she felt had lingered on her for several seconds. Instead of explaining her thoughts, she shrugged, having no real answers for him.

He turned back to the sobbing woman. "Do you know where these masked men are now?"

On she sobbed without reply.

Just then, the sound of a blast assaulted Liliana's ears. The ground beneath her feet quaked. She stumbled, grabbing on to Arhyen's arm for balance.

The woman wailed louder.

Ephraim, Liliana, and Arhyen all looked at each other, nodded, then took off full speed toward the general direction of the explosion.

Liliana paced herself as usual to ensure the men

would not fall behind, but Arhyen had no trouble keeping up. Soon they both had to slow for Ephraim to reach them. Together they all jogged out onto Market Street, now mostly cleared of its inhabitants, barring a few sobbing or otherwise delusional people stumbling about.

Most of the storefronts seemed unharmed, except for a few instances of broken glass, just as likely to have been caused by those infected by the emotions as the terrorists.

"Keep running," Arhyen instructed as she began to slow, observing the remaining people in the streets.

She glanced at him, then peered past his outstretched finger. "Is that-" she began.

"Watch Headquarters," Ephraim's voice trembled. He slowed his jog to a walk. He scanned the street around them, but there was nothing to see except the infected people.

The ruined building smoldered across the street. Some of the walls still partially remained, but the rest was rubble, both inside and out. Huge chunks of brick littered the street. A few flames licked at the splintered furniture and broken boards, adding to the vast amount of smoke in the air.

Ephraim kicked a charred piece of brick at his feet.

"You could have been in there!" Liliana gasped, her eyes riveted to him. "What was Hamlet thinking?" As soon as she said it, she realized what a silly statement it was. Hamlet was only thinking of his plan, he would not care if Ephraim was killed.

"Christoph was connected to one of the LN's splinter groups," Ephraim stated blandly. "Perhaps the LN had operatives on the inside watching him. The Queen's Guard's involvement with the LN only increases that likelihood. It makes sense that Hamlet would target Watch Headquarters. Now we only need to deduce where he will strike next."

Liliana watched Ephraim's expression, waiting for signs of emotion to dawn. The annihilated building might have contained several of his colleagues. Several of his *friends*.

Still gazing at the ruined building, his expression crumbled.

Noticing, Arhyen stepped toward him. "We should check for survivors," he said softly.

Liliana nodded in agreement, though she knew there could be no survivors with such a large explosion. It had utterly obliterated the building, taking most of the surrounding two buildings with it. She didn't want to march forward and see what had become of the bodies. With such an impact they would hardly be recognizable.

Ephraim shook his head sharply, seeming to regain his composure. "There is no time. We must intervene before more are killed."

Out of nowhere, a man came barreling toward them, aiming a metal pipe at the back of Ephraim's head. Ephraim began to turn, but would be too late. Jumping into motion, she lunged to intercept the man, but Arhyen somehow beat her to it, launching a miraculous kick at the man's side, sending him off course. The man stumbled, dropping his pipe, giving Ephraim the time to turn and knock him in the head with the butt of his pistol. The man fell to the ground, motionless.

Barely able to comprehend what had just happened, Liliana stared at Arhyen, gazing down at the unconscious man in disbelief.

Slowly, he raised his horrified eyes to her. "I'm like

them now, aren't I? Like Hazel and the other men she experimented on."

She swallowed the lump in her throat. He had moved too quickly for a human. She knew it had been Hazel's aim to make him like her, but she'd only had Arhyen for a short time. Had she managed to alter him to such a great extent, or had the London Network added to the damage in their time with him? With a sad smile, she nodded. "Yes, I dare say you are."

Ephraim grunted angrily, kicking the man's dropped pipe to send it clattering a few paces down the street. He turned rage-filled eyes back to the smoldering ruins of Watch Headquarters. "Bloody automatons," he grumbled, then stalked toward the building's remains.

Arhyen moved to Liliana's side. He took her hand and gave it a squeeze. She had a million things she wanted to say, a million fears to express, but she remained silent, for in that moment she felt Arhyen was just as frightened as she, if not more so.

❧

LOOKING AMONGST THE DEBRIS, ARHYEN CLENCHED his hands in frustration. It was near impossible to closely examine the remains of Watch Headquarters. The rubble was still smoldering, and the building's frame slumped perilously, still partially standing . . . for now. They'd searched the streets around the ruined building for signs of evidence, but the search was fruitless. The bodies had been rendered unidentifiable, and whatever had caused the explosion was destroyed entirely in the blast.

He gazed out at the street. There was hardly a soul left in the area, save a few crying people, and more than a few corpses. He tried hard to avoid gazing closely at them. He didn't want to recognize anyone among the dead.

"We should move on," Ephraim muttered. "We need to figure out where he'll strike next if we hope to stand a chance of stopping him."

Liliana had stopped walking to peer down at one of the bodies killed in the explosion.

He approached and put his hand on her shoulder, cringing as she startled at his touch.

She blinked up at him, then turned her gaze to Ephraim. "Or maybe we just need to figure out where he'll strike last."

Arhyen looked down at her in confusion. "What do you mean?" he pressed.

She gazed up at the sky, slowly growing dim. "It will be night soon, and Hamlet has already caused so much destruction. He told me everything would be over in three days. If today counts as the third day, then it will end at midnight. We have to figure out where it will end."

Arhyen sucked his teeth, digesting what she was saying. They were running out of time. *He* was running out of time. If he didn't come through on his part of the bargain, the LN would come after him, and anyone associated with him, leverage be damned.

"We risk him striking somewhere else before this . . . finale," Ephraim observed as he approached.

"We're not likely to guess his next strike regardless," Liliana countered. "Our best chance lies in preventing his final move."

"And you think you know this final move?" Ephraim pressed, stroking his chin in thought.

She nodded. "Buckingham Palace. It has to be. He's already attacked the Market District, and if the rumors are true, London Bridge. Nothing could be a larger finale than the palace."

Arhyen felt like a fool for not thinking of it sooner. He gazed out at the surrounding destruction, likely just a small taste of what was to come. "You're right. If he's striking against the London Network, and the London Network belongs to the Queen, *she* will be the finale."

"Then we should get moving," Ephraim replied, glancing around the mostly still street. "I don't think we'll be catching any carriages today." He turned his gaze back to the rubble at his feet, his expression unreadable.

Arhyen thought about offering comfort, but he knew for a fact it would not be appreciated. Liliana gazed at Ephraim longingly, seeming to have come to the same conclusion.

Ephraim turned back, glaring at both of them. "Let's go. I'm ready to send that automaton back to hell where he belongs."

They nodded.

Arhyen stole another glance at Liliana as they departed. Her worried expression matched his. It was all well and good to decide it was time to end Hamlet's reign of terror. It was quite another thing to actually do it, and survive.

CHAPTER 9

"I wish we could have visited Buckingham Palace under better circumstances," Liliana admitted, hoping to break the heavy silence.

They'd entered the industrial district, cautiously scanning the eerily empty streets. The surrounding mills and warehouses were utterly still. Liliana didn't like the silence. She could hear screams and chaos in other areas of the city, but not here. Here, there was only the delicate sound of water dripping from rooftops, and the occasional scrabble and subsequent flutter of a pigeon looking for food.

"Why is it so quiet?" she asked when nobody responded to her first statement

"The hardworking folk are likely hiding in their homes," Ephraim explained, keeping his gaze forward as he walked. "And the looters have no business in this part of town. Now that the chaos has died down on Market Street, they will begin to swarm, hoping to take advantage of tragedy."

"That's awful," she muttered, thinking back to the ruined buildings and dead bodies. How anyone could hope to benefit from such terror was beyond her.

"What's awful is that they're put into the position to loot in the first place," Arhyen argued. "It's not their fault they were born into lives where their next meal was never guaranteed. They survive any way they can."

"Spoken like a true thief," Ephraim replied caustically. "Blame the system, and not the criminal. Everyone chooses their own path. There is no excuse."

"Spoken like someone who's never gone hungry," Arhyen replied with a growl.

"Please," Liliana interrupted, growing nervous that an argument was about to ensue. "Now is not the time for this."

Ephraim glared at her, so she held her tongue.

With a second glance, his expression softened. "I apologize, I seem to be a bit . . . emotional at the moment."

Arhyen moved to Ephraim's side and placed a hand on his shoulder. Ephraim sighed, then met his gaze, nodded, and the argument seemed to be over.

Liliana smirked. She would never understand men.

They had only walked a few more steps when Arhyen whispered, "Don't look now, but someone is watching us."

Liliana tensed, barely breathing. She resisted the urge to look around. She sidled up to Arhyen as his pace slowed.

"It might be the London Network," he continued in a whisper. "I would not be surprised if they sent someone to make sure I came through on my part of the bargain. Just keep walking."

They resumed a steady pace.

Liliana tried to act casual, but she feared the newly acquired stiffness in her gait would give her away. She risked a glance toward a side alley and gasped.

"I don't think it's the LN," she whispered. "I just saw someone in a mask."

"Hamlet?" Arhyen questioned softly, not missing a step.

She shook her head. "Too short to be him, though the mask was the same."

"One of his accomplices then," Ephraim quietly observed.

"What do you think they want?" she questioned. She was growing increasingly nervous, wondering if she could catch this masked person before they could escape . . . but what if there was more than one?

Arhyen glanced over at her. "Likely sent to watch *you*," he replied, his voice barely audible.

Making the decision for her, he suddenly darted backward, then ran toward the alley where she'd seen the masked form.

Liliana was about to follow him, when she saw another figure, also wearing a mask, peeking out from the intersection ahead. Judging from just a brief glimpse, she concluded this one was not Hamlet either, and was likely female.

"There's another," Ephraim grumbled, peering to his left as Liliana caught a brief glimpse of a third form. His hand gravitated toward his pistol.

Liliana was about to reach out and stop him from firing on the masked form, then a crashing noise sounded from the alleyway where Arhyen had disappeared. Quickly making up her mind, Liliana left Ephraim to his own devices in favor of helping Arhyen.

She raced back down the street, then veered into the

alleyway, blindly rushing ahead. She skidded to a halt, her heart dropping to her feet as she found Arhyen, lying on his back on a pile of broken crates. Time slowed as she hesitantly stepped toward his still form, then he groaned, and time started back up again. She knelt by his side, peering down at his face.

His eyes opened to blink up at her. "That might not have been Hamlet," he groaned, lifting his hand to his forehead, "but it was definitely another automaton."

She glanced both ways down the alley, but the masked culprit had disappeared. In her perusal she spotted Arhyen's hat a few paces away, and stood to retrieve it, but froze as pistol fire sounded from the main street.

"Ephraim," she gasped. She tossed Arhyen's hat to him, then raced back out onto the street.

She sped back in the direction she'd come, worried Ephraim had shot someone, or worse, *he'd* been shot, but she was not expecting what she found. A masked form lay in the street in a growing pool of blood from a chest wound. Ephraim stood a few paces away, peering speculatively at a man wearing the same uniform as the ones they'd found dead on Tailor Street. A member of the Queen's Guard, if she wasn't mistaken.

Arhyen stumbled up behind her. "Wakefield?" he questioned.

The uniformed man turned his cool gaze toward Arhyen and Liliana. He seemed to be frowning, though it was difficult to tell if it was just the weighty effect of his full gray moustache.

Before he could reply, three more uniformed men trotted toward them from the nearest intersection. Upon arrival, one complained, "The rest have escaped."

Ephraim took a few steps back, reaching Arhyen and

Liliana. "Would someone care to explain what the hell is going on here?"

Wakefield gazed at him for several seconds, then turned to Arhyen. "I sincerely hope you are not working with these masked fiends," he accused, venom clear in his tone.

Liliana observed each of the uniformed men, doing her best to memorize their features. Were these the men who had held Arhyen captive? He'd known the gray-haired one by name.

"They were following us," Arhyen explained. "I fully intend to come through on my half of the bargain."

"That better be true," the gray-haired man, Wakefield, growled. He turned back to his men. "Comb the streets again, make sure no one else lingers." He glanced down at the corpse near his boots as his men set their feet into motion. He snatched the sleeve of one before he could trot away. "Hide the body for later observation. I want to know what Hamlet has done to these men."

The man nodded, and stooped to the corpse. Gripping its upper arms, he began dragging the body away.

"So he *does* have others working for him," Arhyen concluded thoughtfully.

Wakefield flicked his gaze first to Ephraim, then to Liliana, before finally settling back on Arhyen. "As do you, but enough of this. We're clearly running out of time. I'm finding it unlikely that you'll be able to stop what's happening before Codename Hamlet is through, so I can only hope I survive long enough to hunt you and your associates down once you fail."

He turned and marched away after his men, joining the one attempting to pull the corpse. He lifted the corpse's feet, and together they carried it out of sight.

"Hunt us down?" Liliana questioned. "What about your leverage?"

"Hamlet has already exposed your father's synthetic emotions," Arhyen explained. "If he finishes what he's started, my leverage will not matter. Our only choice will be to flee London."

"Or to utterly eliminate the LN," Ephraim observed, "which it seems Hamlet might actually accomplish."

Liliana's eyes widened at the thought. Could that really be possible? If the LN was gone, perhaps she, Arhyen, and Ephraim would be safe. Of course, it would be at the cost of countless other lives. She shook her head lightly, unable to stomach the sacrifice.

Arhyen's worried gaze lingered on her. Fearing he'd read her thoughts on her face, she met his gaze with apprehension.

He abruptly reached out and pulled her into a hug, then kissed the top of her head. "Wakefield knows your face now," he muttered. "I should never have brought you along. I can only hope he perishes long before we do."

She swallowed the lump in her throat and returned his embrace. "Unfortunately, I cannot bring myself to wish for another's death," she croaked.

He held her tighter. "I never thought I could either. Then I met you, and realized without a doubt, that I will always put your life first."

Tears stung at her eyes as she pulled away. Arhyen was right. It might be selfish, perhaps it was even evil, but she'd always put his life first too.

As they left the industrial district behind, Arhyen realized his legs were not as tired as they should have been, judging by Ephraim's weary state. Ephraim kept up, however, without complaint.

Really, they all should have been jogging. It would soon be dark, and they were running out of time. They needed some form of transportation if they hoped to make it to Buckingham Palace before Hamlet finished his plan. They might already be too late.

He could have told Wakefield their thoughts on Hamlet's finale so he could send his people ahead to the palace, yet, if he had, Wakefield may well have killed them on the spot, deeming them no longer useful. Perhaps it was selfish to risk the fate of the city to protect his own life, but he'd done it all the same. Here was hoping he wouldn't regret it.

"We'll never make it in time," Ephraim panted, giving voice to Arhyen's worries. He stopped walking and removed his fedora to wipe his sweat-slick brow with his sleeve, then lifted his arms over his head to stretch. His back popped, and he cringed. "You two should run ahead without me."

Arhyen met Liliana's nervous gaze.

She nodded. "Do you think you can keep up?"

Could he? He wasn't sure, but he was willing to try.

"Don't worry about me," Ephraim said somewhat sarcastically. "I'll just make my way on my own, with only my pistol to protect me."

Liliana, still looking as fresh as she had that morning, smirked. "You're safer here than we'll be confronting Hamlet. You know full well we wouldn't leave you otherwise."

Arhyen thought he could almost detect a blush on Ephraim's face, though there was no time to mock him for it. He turned back to Liliana. "Let's go."

She nodded, then spared a final glance for Ephraim.

"If we do not see you at the palace, we'll reconvene at the apartment in the morning?"

Arhyen shook his head. "Unwise. If we fail, Wakefield may send men there to find us."

Ephraim smirked. "If we fail, meeting up again will be the least of our concerns."

Liliana opened her mouth to argue, but Arhyen placed a hand on her arm. They were running out of time, and Ephraim was right. If they failed . . . he shook his head. Thinking about it now would do them little good.

"Let's go," he coaxed, still holding onto Liliana's arm.

She frowned, but nodded, and they both began to run, leaving Ephraim behind. Liliana kept a few steps behind him since only he knew the way to Buckingham Palace. They ran past the last three blocks of factories, and into the old wealthy district. Most of the homes had fallen into disrepair, long since abandoned for the more trendy district of White Heights.

Arhyen never stopped scanning the area for white masked figures, though it seemed the Queen's Guard had scared them off. Still, why were they following them in the first place? Had Hamlet sent them to keep Liliana out of trouble, or did he know they were coming for him? At least one of the men, the one he'd confronted in the alley, had been an automaton. For all he knew, Hamlet had an entire army of automatons, and perhaps others who'd been experimented on like himself. Perhaps he'd even recruited some of Hazel's leftover followers.

He shuddered as his feet splashed through a muddy puddle. If that was the case, they stood little chance of succeeding. Just facing Hamlet was risky enough. He'd managed to slaughter an entire farm building full of half automaton men on his own. Though he'd sustained serious injuries in return, he was still a more than formidable foe. One Arhyen secretly hoped he would never have to face. He already knew what the result would be.

"People," Liliana observed, pointing to one of the nearby mansions.

He slowed to a jog to observe a group of seemingly poor folk huddled near the front of the decrepit building, while a large man attempted to break down the door.

"Looking for a place to hide," he observed. "We should leave them be."

"What if they know something?" she questioned softly, her voice hitching as her feet rhythmically pounded the cobblestones.

"There's no time," he replied. "We must stick to our plan. Reach the palace and find Hamlet."

He didn't miss her hesitant nod, nor the way her fingers brushed her coat pocket where the small vial of poison hid. He knew she didn't want to kill Hamlet, but there was no other choice.

"How do you intend to make him drink?" he asked abruptly.

She nearly stumbled before righting herself to continue jogging. They were beginning to see more and more people, all scared, some injured, some shaking and seeming to recover from the effects of synthetic emotions. They likely thought the worse was over now. How wrong they were.

"I don't know," she answered finally, tucking a stray lock of red hair back under her cap as she jogged. "I've been trying to think of a way, but-"

"But you don't want to do it," he finished for her.

She turned wide eyes to him, then quickly averted her gaze.

"It's alright," he pressed. "I know you're not the killing type."

She stopped running, forcing Arhyen to halt beside her. "It's not just that," she blurted. "I just don't want to kill him! I know he's done horrible things. He killed my father, and now he's destroying the city, but I understand why he's doing it. He did not choose this life. It just doesn't seem fair!"

Arhyen was at a complete loss for words. He'd noted her hesitation to harm Hamlet from the start, but he'd never expected her to be on his side in all this.

"Liliana," he began patiently. "He's killing innocent people."

Tears began to fall down her face, making her blue eyes sparkle. "I know. I know what he's doing, but he has also saved my life. He saved *yours* too. And Ephraim's. Do we owe him nothing?"

"Perhaps we do owe him," he sighed, anxious to get moving. Some of the gathering crowd were beginning to stare at them arguing in the middle of the empty street.

"Then *how* can we kill him!" she cried.

He shook his head. "It's what we have to do to survive. If we do not stop him, the London Network will come after all of us. If we do not stop him, we both will die."

"There must be another way!" she began to sob. "Perhaps he can be reasoned with. He's listened to me before."

Arhyen opened his mouth to argue, then his eyes opened wider. Behind Liliana approached an entire group of masked figures, all clad in black.

The figure at the front of the group stepped forward. "How touching," he observed in his cultured tone.

Liliana gasped, then whipped around. "Hamlet!"

He removed his black top hat, then swooped down into a bow. His minions remained silently standing behind him.

Raising from his bow, he took another step forward. "I'm glad to see you well, Mr. Croft, though I had advised Ms. Breckenridge to let you stay put."

Arhyen scowled. "Do not blame her. I got out on my own."

Gazing at Hamlet, Liliana stammered, "D-did you-"

"Hear everything?" Hamlet questioned. "Why yes. You know I have impeccable hearing." He turned back to his minions. "Half of you go keep a look out," he instructed. "Time is short, and I do not want to be interrupted."

Arhyen watched four of his minions trot away, leaving four behind, plus Hamlet. Nervous sweat began to bead on his brow, though it was freezing outside. If Hamlet knew they intended to kill him, then . . .

Hamlet took another step forward. "I must advise you both to return to Mr. Croft's apartment. I assure you, come morning, you will not be in danger . . . at least not from the London Network."

Arhyen moved to place himself in front of Liliana. "For some reason, I do not find that comforting."

Hamlet chuckled. "You honestly think I would harm her, after the pains I have suffered to keep her alive?"

Not trusting Hamlet's words, he took another step, shielding Liliana with his body.

"I implore you to step aside, Mr. Croft," Hamlet stated calmly, eerily tilting his masked face as he observed them. "I would have a word with Ms. Breckinridge before I depart."

He debated taking Liliana's hand and running, but knew he could not. This might be their last chance to stop Hamlet, and she could handle herself. Grudgingly, he stepped aside, then quickly met Liliana's gaze, beseeching her. Once Hamlet was close, they could shove the poison down his throat.

Hamlet took several more steps forward, placing himself within reach of both Arhyen and Liliana. Arhyen's skin broke out in goosebumps. If Hamlet laid a finger on Liliana, he would kill him himself, poison or no.

"I hear you have something you'd like me to drink," Hamlet said curiously.

Arhyen attempted to hide his surprise. He really had heard *everything*. Had he been following them just out of sight the entire time?

He watched as Liliana blinked up at Hamlet.

Please, just give it to him, he thought, unable to speak his wishes out loud. Perhaps Hamlet didn't understand that the liquid within the vial would paralyze him.

Liliana glanced at Arhyen, then bit her lip as she turned back to Hamlet. "Please, just stop what you're doing. You're killing innocent people."

"No one is innocent," Hamlet scoffed, straightening his top hat. "Do you think any of these so-called innocent people would even spare you a glance if they knew what you are?"

"Th-that doesn't matter," she stammered. "They do not deserve to die, simply for not understanding."

"Show me the vial in your pocket," he instructed, ignoring her argument.

"Leave her alone," Arhyen interrupted. "You're frightening her." *If she gives him that vial*, he thought, *we're finished*.

Hamlet snickered. "Oh, methinks our dear Liliana does not frighten so easily." He turned back to her. "Now please, give me the vial."

Arhyen watched on in horror as she lifted a trembling hand to her pocket and withdrew the vial. She stole a glance down at the black liquid, then handed it to Hamlet.

He received it with his black gloved hand, popping the lid off with his thumb. He held it up to the gray sky and peered at the liquid, then lowered his gaze to Liliana. "Would you like me to drink it?"

Arhyen froze. Did he really not understand what it was? Was he so trusting of Liliana that he believed she would never dream of poisoning him?

He watched as tears began to fall down her face, and knew she'd never be able to go through with it. He was surprised to realize he didn't blame her. He could never fault her for having more compassion than anyone he'd ever met, even if it was misguided.

Hamlet lowered the vial. "Please, do not cry. I did not mean to upset you. I was simply asking if it is your wish for me to drink the contents of this vial."

Liliana shook her head over and over. "You don't understand," she blurted, "what's in the vial will paralyze you. The LN gave it to us to kill you."

Hamlet stared down at her for several heartbeats.

Arhyen tensed, prepared for a violent reaction.

Instead, Hamlet took on an easy stance, the uncapped vial still in his hand. "Yes. My apologies for eavesdropping. I know the purpose of this poison." He lifted the vial in salute, like one would when sharing a drink with friends. "My question to you is, would like me to drink it?"

"I don't understand," Liliana gasped, the tears still steadily flowing down her face.

"If you do not want me to finish my grand plan,"

Hamlet began, "then I will drink this vial. Truly, I have nothing to live for if I cannot have my revenge."

Arhyen gritted his jaw in frustration. Hamlet was toying with her. He'd never *actually* drink the poison.

"I don't want you to finish your plan," she breathed.

Hamlet nodded, then lifted the bottom edge of his mask enough to reveal brutally scarred skin. He lifted the vial toward his lips, somehow spared the scarring that consumed most of his chin and lower cheeks.

"But I do not want you to drink what's in the vial!" Liliana shouted, reaching for him.

Arhyen's mind was spinning with adrenaline as Hamlet lowered the vial, then his mask. His remaining minions muttered amongst themselves in confusion.

"Either I drink the vial, or I finish my plan," Hamlet explained. "There is no other choice."

Liliana buried her face in her hands and continued to cry. "This should not be my choice," she sobbed. "Please, do not make me choose."

"Liliana," Arhyen began, placing his hand gently on her shoulder.

"No!" she cried, pulling away. "I know what you would have me do, but I cannot."

He approached her again while Hamlet watched on. "If you choose to let him go, I will not fault you for it," he assured. "It's alright."

She lifted her face from her palms and peered up at him with red-rimmed eyes. She met his gaze for several seconds. Seeming to have gained her final answer from his expression, she marched up to Hamlet, took the vial from his grasp, then dumped it on the cobblestones.

"If you continue with your plan I will be forced to stop you by any means necessary," she stated boldly, "but I will not cause your death when there is still hope of saving you. This choice is yours, not mine, and you cannot force me to make it for you."

Hamlet watched her for several seconds, then inclined his head. "So be it." He turned to Arhyen. "I would bid you adieu, Mr. Croft, but I believe the proper parting words in this situation are, *see you soon*."

With that, he turned away, gesturing for his minions to follow.

Arhyen debated going after him and sticking a knife in his back. He glanced at the black liquid pooling around the cobblestones.

"I-I just couldn't do it," Liliana continued to sob. She looked up at him pleadingly. "I'm s-sorry."

He pulled her close and wrapped her in his arms, only then noticing that their onlookers had fled at the appearance of the masked men. "He was only toying with you," he assured. "He never would have willingly drank poison."

He was glad Liliana couldn't see his face, because he really wasn't sure about his statement. Would Hamlet have willingly given in, if only Liliana had asked?

Either way, he'd made it clear that death was the only thing that would stop him from finishing his plan.

He held Liliana close as she cried, trembling like an injured bird. It was now clear to him that he would be stopping Hamlet on his own, or at the very least, he would die trying.

❧

LILIANA FINALLY MANAGED TO QUIET HER TEARS, BUT found herself reluctant to pull away from Arhyen. At that moment, safe within the circle of his arms, she could pretend she hadn't just doomed all of London. She knew

Hamlet deserved to die, and that his death would prevent the deaths of many others, yet she'd still failed. Perhaps *she* was the one who deserved to die.

Arhyen's arms around her loosened, then he slowly pulled away to peer down at her with his kind brown eyes. "I want you to return to the apartment," he instructed.

Shocked, she pulled away from him.

"I should never have put you in this position," he continued. "I knew you didn't have it in your heart to kill him, and it was wrong of me to place that burden upon you. I only thought-"

"That I was the best chance of getting him to take it," she finished for him. "And you were right. I didn't even have to force it upon him. He offered to take it, and I said no. I've doomed us all."

He gripped her shoulders and gazed into her eyes. "You haven't doomed anyone. I will stop him. You will return to the apartment where it's safe. I want you to lock the door behind you, and do not emerge until I return."

She felt sick at the thought of separating. She'd already thought she'd lost him too many times, and she could not bear another. "He'll kill you!" she argued. "I cannot let you go alone. Surely, if he's about to harm others, I will not hesitate. If he's about to harm *you*, I know I will not."

"Liliana," he began again calmly. "Please just go home. Do not worry about me."

"That's like asking the sun not to shine," she blurted, realizing she hadn't chosen the best analogy, considering the sun had been blotted out by heavy clouds all day, and now was barely visible even as it set.

He released her arms. "I'm not taking you to Buckingham Palace," he began again. "Either you go home, or we'll both wait here until Hamlet finishes what he started."

She stared at him for several seconds, hoping to call his bluff, but his gaze did not relent.

"You wouldn't," she accused.

"I would," he continued. "I'd rather have to save you from the London Network tomorrow, than force you to do something that would break your heart, because I can see now, that's exactly what killing Hamlet would do to you."

"It would not!" she gasped. "I can handle it."

He shook his head. "I like to think that perhaps your heart is mine to protect. If it is, then I believe that is my primary duty. So please, go home."

Her mind was churning like an angry river. How could he just tell her to go? "We're running out of time," she urged.

With a patient look on his face, he crossed his arms, waiting for her to make up her mind.

"You can't do this," she insisted, but he simply continued to wait. She could see there would be no convincing him.

"Fine," she breathed. "Just go before it's too late. I'll go home."

Almost too fast for her to react, he grabbed her again and kissed her so passionately it stole her breath. She returned the kiss, fighting the tears stinging the corners of her eyes.

He pulled away and gave her the most heart-wrenching look she'd ever seen, then turned and ran in the direction Hamlet and the others had gone.

She watched his back until it grew small enough to disappear, then counted to ten before surveying the street around her. Now where had those people gone? Surely one of them could tell her how to get to Buckingham Palace.

Arhyen might be much faster than he used to be, but he still wasn't faster than her.

CHAPTER 10

Arhyen pumped his legs as fast as he could, which was considerably faster than he thought himself capable. Darkness had fallen, and unfortunately his eyes didn't seem any better than they'd been before. It was difficult to see without the street lamps of the more populous areas of the city.

He pushed his legs faster. He was no Liliana, but he hoped he could reach Buckingham Palace in time to stop Hamlet. *How* he would do that, he was not sure. He could barely gather his thoughts enough to concoct a new plan. His mind continuously flashed back to Liliana's tear-streaked face. Had he been wrong to send her home? He didn't like her being out on her own, but the same logic applied to her as it did to Ephraim. Whoever reached the palace first was the one in most danger. *He* would be the one in danger, not Liliana, and that was how he wanted it.

Still, he wished he at least had a pistol or *anything* to stop Hamlet from a distance. He was skilled at throwing knives, but he doubted a blade or two would even slow him.

He was so lost in his thoughts that he almost didn't notice the crowd gathering in the dark street ahead. They were in a residential area, surrounded by full districts of eerie silence, save the occasional scream, or breaking of glass as looters took what they pleased. Some members of the crowd held hastily made torches, the flickering light illuminating their coat clad backs.

He debated even checking to see what had drawn the crowd, but on the off chance it was something that could help him defeat Hamlet, he slowed.

Reaching the crowd, he pushed forward through the outer ring, then soon heard what had drawn everyone's attention.

"This is our opportunity!" a man shouted from the front line. "London is in chaos, now it's time for us to stop playing the victims!"

A bad feeling permeated Arhyen's gut. He pushed forward until he could see who spoke. He didn't recognize the man, but he wore a plain heavy coat, and tan trousers tucked into stovepipe boots, marking him a common working man, likely a mill employee.

"Now is the time to take back the respect we deserve!" he shouted, pumping his fist in the air.

The crowd shouted their agreement, pumping their fists. Some brandished weapons, holding them high like war trophies.

Now fully understanding the crowd's purpose, Arhyen slowly backed away. This was not the time to get caught up in a mob. Some of the men and women gathered eyed him suspiciously as he backed away, so he stopped and gave a few half-hearted fist pumps of his own.

The leader shouted something else he couldn't quite

hear over the murmuring crowd, then everyone began marching forward. More shoddy torches were lit one by one, engulfing the crowd in their angry light.

Arhyen was shoved along with the moving crowd. He kept a slow pace, hoping they would all soon surpass him, and he could slip away into the darkness without having the angry mob turn on him.

"To the palace!" the mob leader shouted, echoed by the crowd.

That gave him pause. An angry mob might be of use to him, they might distract Hamlet so he could . . . no, they were moving too slowly. They would likely arrive long after Hamlet had finished his work. He needed to slip away.

He tried to lag further behind, but almost immediately someone shoved him forward. He glared over his shoulder at the culprit, then quickly turned back around. He might have to take his chances with a fight, but preferably not with a massive sailor, his tattooed arms bare to the cold. He was only part automaton, and most of the crowd was armed. Some might even have pistols, though they were illegal for civilians.

He bit his lip in frustration, then clamped down too hard as someone else shoved him. He tasted blood in his mouth. It was time to make a run for it.

He turned to go, but was met by a torch wielding woman with a fierce gaze, and a butcher knife in her free hand. She towered over him, her wide frame blocking any possible route of escape. She sneered, showcasing her numerous missing teeth.

With a gulp, Arhyen turned back around. If he couldn't escape out the back, perhaps he could work his way to the side and slip away then.

He was jostled around, slowly making his way across,

then was nearly thrown to the ground as someone shouted, "Halt!"

The crowd abruptly stopped moving, those in the back bumping into those ahead of them. He looked around for an escape route, but the bodies around him were packed too tightly. He'd have to shove his way through.

"By order of the Queen!" someone shouted, "You are all under arrest!"

Well *shit*. He hopped on tip toe until he caught sight of a whole troop of the Queen's Guard illuminated by hand-held lanterns, preparing to circle the mob.

"We will not be put down!" the mob leader shouted. As one, they surged forward, carrying Arhyen forward with them.

He frantically tried to work his way backward, no longer caring if the mob turned on him. He could not risk arrest when he needed to *meet* with Hamlet.

He heard a metallic clang, then someone screamed. Someone in the mob must have attacked one of the Queen's Guard, or perhaps it was the other way around. Thoroughly done with the situation, he dropped to his knees and began to crawl past people's legs. He got kicked and kneed a few times, but eventually he made it to the edge of the crowd. Not even bothering to look for signs of danger, he stood and started running back in the direction he'd come.

"Halt!" someone called, likely a member of the Guard, but he didn't look back.

He ran on into the darkness, plotting the city in his head for the next shortest route to the palace. He should never have joined the crowd. He'd lost too much time. If he wasn't going to be too late before, surely he was now.

❧

Liliana ran as fast as her legs would carry her, glad to be in her trousers instead of an encumbering dress. It had taken her several attempts to actually find someone who would speak with her, but now she had directions to the palace in her head, along with a few areas to avoid where angry mobs were seen gathering.

Darkness had fallen, but it didn't slow her. She could see as well in the dark as most nocturnal animals, perhaps better. She knew she'd promised Arhyen she'd go home, and she never wanted to break a promise to him, but some things were greater than personal honor. She could not let him face Hamlet alone.

As she ran, she found herself desperately wishing Ephraim had been able to keep up with them. His cool, calm presence was what she really could have used in that moment, and she was sure Arhyen would benefit too. She and Arhyen were different in many ways, but they both tended to lead with instinct and emotion. They took uncalculated risks, whereas Ephraim viewed everything from a logical stance. If they were going to stop Hamlet from finishing his plan, while also avoiding the Queen's Guard, the LN, and Hamlet's minions, they needed logic. Ephraim had probably figured out Hamlet's entire plan already, but he was too slow physically to do anything about it.

So, alas, she didn't have Ephraim, and if she beat Arhyen to the palace, she wouldn't have him either. It was all up to her, and she had no idea what to do. She'd already tried to reason with Hamlet, and she'd been unable to poison him. Now it seemed her only real option was to fight him. She'd proven that perhaps she didn't have the heart to kill him, but she suspected he also didn't have the heart to kill her. That was her only advantage.

She rounded another dark street corner. She could hear angry shouting in the distance, and a few screams. Occasionally someone hiding from the chaos would scurry past her on the street, or she'd catch sight of looters carrying big canvas sacks or large crates. She saw no officers of the Queen's Guard, nor any of the Watch. She knew Hamlet couldn't have possibly killed them all, but they were likely busy in other parts of the city. She briefly wondered how many might be protecting the palace, then she skidded to a halt. There it was.

In the distance she could see a massive rectangular building with a row of stone pillars decorating the foreground. Street lamps lined the heavy iron gate encircling the entire structure, gently lighting the pillars and building beyond. She could see guards posted around the entirety of the gate, and countless more around the actual building. They all stood at quiet attention as if nothing was amiss, but their numbers portended the Queen was well aware of the events taking place in the city.

She scurried closer, hiding behind small hedges in the green across the street. Once she was close enough to clearly see each of the guards around the gate, she paused her advance, lest she alert them.

Crouching low to the ground, she scanned the massive palace for signs of Hamlet or his henchmen. If he was there already, he'd somehow gotten past all the guards without alerting them. The other option, she gulped, was that they'd been wrong, and Hamlet had no intention of attacking the palace. He'd never confirmed that his finale would occur there, they'd just assumed.

Now, staring at the silent guards, she was beginning to think they'd been wrong.

She was just preparing to turn around to go find Arhyen when her eye caught a brief hint of movement on the palace roof. She resumed her low crouch and stared at the point where she'd seen the movement. She was lucky the clouds had rescinded, letting the moon shine through onto the roof, else she likely wouldn't have noticed it at all.

There. There was clearly someone walking along the roof, just a single figure. Could it be Hamlet? Would his finale take place without the aid of his minions? She supposed they could be elsewhere, and she supposed it really didn't matter. Her eyes were glued to the solitary figure on the rooftop, and she knew without a doubt that she must find her way up there before it was too late.

She forced her gaze away from the figure and back to the guards lining the gate. How could she get past them without being seen? She supposed she could alert them all that there was a terrorist on the roof, but she suspected that would not end well for anyone. No, her best chance was to catch Hamlet alone, without a bevy of guards forcing him to act.

She scanned the line of guards once more, then quickly decided there was no way she was getting in the front gate. Perhaps around the back. She retreated far enough to not be spotted, then began making her way around. Eventually she reached the far end of the gated palace, which provided a more interesting option.

A long lake dominated a green park, leading up to a broad manicured strip of land bordering the actual building. The gate still continued all around, but the guards were fewer on this end, likely believing threats would not be coming from the water. They watched the gate at either end of the lake, but none were posted near the sandy bank. If anyone tried to approach the palace on one of the many boats moored along the waterway, they would still be seen long before they reached the shore, but few would expect a threat coming from *beneath* the water's surface.

She took a nervous breath, scanning the dark choppy waters. She was no fine swimmer. In fact, the only time she'd ever been in such a large amount of water was with Hamlet, and he'd carried her across on his shoulders. She'd very likely drown before making it all the way across . . . but as far as she could tell, it was her only option. She was running out of time.

Her mind made up, she quickly scaled the unguarded fence surrounding the waterway, crouching low as she edged toward the bank and moored boats to her left. If only she could hop into one of the boats instead of into the icy black water. Who knew what could be dwelling beneath its surface?

Trembling with apprehension, she slipped into the water, gasping as the frigid temperature hit her. Now she knew another reason the waterway wasn't heavily guarded. Anyone trying to swim across would likely freeze long before they made it.

She inched further into the water until it reached her throat, and her feet could no longer touch the bottom. She paddled her arms, bobbing gently up and down. Fortunately, she didn't have the chaotic current to deal with here like she and Hamlet had in the Thames. She was able to maintain her position long enough to figure out how to float. She gave a few experimental kicks, propelling herself further across the water, being careful not to let her feet break the surface, lest one of the guards hear her splash.

This wasn't so bad. At least she didn't feel like she was about to drown.

She pushed onward at a snail's pace, keeping her head barely above the surface. In the dark night, the guards would never be able to see her. With increasing confidence, she gently paddled on.

By the time she was halfway across the lake, her clothing had become a nuisance, especially her coat, yet she could not remove it. Though she'd lost the poison vial, she still had the blue vial in another pocket, Arhyen's leverage. If she lost the coat, she'd lose that too, and she didn't feel her icy hands capable of removing the vial to place in her trouser pocket.

Letting go of the idea of disencumbering herself, she paddled onward.

Time ticked by slowly. Though the cold wasn't unbearable for her, her movements felt sluggish, perhaps a result of her blood slowing in her veins. Keeping her head barely above water, she scanned the distant roofline of the palace. She saw no movement there. Had Hamlet gone inside? If that was the case, she had no idea how she'd find him in time. The palace was massive. There had to be hundreds of rooms.

Cursing her slow strokes, she paddled on.

Finally, just when she thought her limbs would refuse to move any further, she reached the opposite bank. She crawled up onto dry land and huddled there for several minutes, though she only seemed to grow colder now that the icy air was hitting her wet clothing. She found herself almost hoping Hamlet *had* gone inside. It would at least be warm in there.

First thing was first though, she had to get up on the roof. Arhyen had started running for the palace before her, so even though he wasn't quite as fast, he should be arriving there soon. She needed to end this before he did.

She began forcing herself to stand, then froze.

"What is that?" a voice called out.

"Torches," another said. "They're coming this way."

She exhaled in relief, realizing the guards were seeing something on the other side of the palace, not the wet freezing girl on the bank. She struggled the rest of the way to standing, then hurried forward, anxious to get the blood flowing to her limbs.

Guards at the palace front shouted to the guards at the back for aid. Liliana sighed in relief, watching the sentries blocking her way hurry around to the front to see what was amiss. She didn't know who the torch wielders were, but they couldn't have had more perfect timing. She hurried up the rocky bank, then over another fence, and soon enough she had her back pressed against the palace wall, glancing about frantically for a way up to the roof.

She peered up at the palace wall hesitantly. There were three horizontal rows of windows, one for each floor, which presented the best handholds. Unfortunately, each window was taller than her. She could make it to the bottom ledge of the middle row of windows easily enough, but hopping up from there to the next would prove difficult. Still, she had to try.

She could hear more guards shouting from the front, and could see no other guards near her. Now was her only chance. Her coat, trousers, and hair dripping water, she turned around and began to scale the building, holding on to narrow ledges with the tips of her fingers. She was overwhelmingly grateful that she'd worn her soft-soled boots. If she'd worn the hard-soled shoes of a proper lady, she never would have made the climb.

Soon enough, she was standing on the ledge of a second story window. Heavy curtains prevented her from seeing anything inside, though the room was dark regardless.

She looked up at the next ledge and inhaled sharply. She'd have to make a jump for it. Wringing the extra moisture that had gathered at the hem of her coat, she crouched in preparation, then sprung upward.

Her body sailed through the air, then her fingertips barely managed to cling to the ledge above. Her body thudded against the window as gravity caught up with her. She remained perfectly still, barely breathing while straining to hold on. The guards still shouted out front. Perhaps she was safe.

She gasped as the window she was leaning against suddenly illuminated. Someone must have heard her thunk and entered the room to assess the cause. She strained her arms to pull herself upward, but was forced to use her feet to scrabble against the window, making more noise.

She nearly fainted in relief as she managed to pull herself up on the ledge, but was once again perilously balanced. She slowly rose and grasped for the ledge above to the third and final window.

The brightness below her increased as someone moved the curtains. Had she taken a moment longer, they would have seen her body dangling right before them. Would they have called the guards to shoot her down?

She shivered, then struggled to slowly pull herself up to the next dark window ledge. Her arms trembling, she took a few seconds to regain her composure.

She pushed back the brim of her cap, dripping residual water down the nape of her neck. She shivered again, then flicked more water from her hem. *Just one more jump*, she thought to herself.

She crouched down, then sprung up, her fingers once again barely catching the edge as she thunked against another window. This time, she did not pause before scurrying her way up. She waited for several heartbeats, but the window below her did not illuminate. She exhaled in relief.

With no more windows to bypass, she took her time finding proper handholds to continue her climb. She was scaling almost sheer wall, just below the edge of the roof, jutting outward above her head. This would be the tough part. She'd only get one chance to swing her arms outward and catch the ledge of the roof. If she couldn't find a handhold, she would fall.

She took a deep breath and thought of Arhyen and Ephraim, and all the other people in London fighting for their lives. If they could survive, so could she.

Gritting her teeth, she flung her arms back just as she pushed off the narrow ledge with her toes. Her hands scrambled for a decent hold that could support the tug she'd feel as gravity caught up with the lower half of her body, but the stones were smooth and slippery. She opened her mouth to scream, then something clamped around her wrist and hauled her upward.

She was lifted through the air until her feet were a few inches above the roof. Hamlet tilted his masked face as he observed her like he'd just caught some sort of strange fish from the sea.

After a moment, he gently set her down on her feet, but she felt so weak and overwhelmed that she instantly crumbled to her knees.

"Greetings, Liliana," he said calmly from above her. "Have you brought more poison for me to drink?"

Panting heavily, she looked up at him. Was he actually being facetious at a time like this? The warmth that she'd built up during the climb was beginning to wear off as the chill wind hit her clothes, making her tired.

She struggled to her feet and removed her cap, cringing as her wet hair slithered down her neck. "No poison," she breathed. "Just a final plea to not finish whatever you're doing. If you do, the London Network will come after Arhyen and everyone he knows."

Hamlet's shoulders slumped as he sighed. "I really wish he would have just stayed put. He could have escaped when my associates attacked the facility where he was being held earlier today. Instead, he had to go and make a deal with the devil."

Liliana's stomach turned. Would it have really been that simple? No. Nothing about this could have ever been simple. Even if Arhyen had escaped during that time, she'd likely still be up on this roof with Hamlet, begging him not to go through with his plan.

"Haven't you proven your point enough?" she began anew. "Surely the London Network has paid for their crimes against you."

"And what of their crimes against *you*, my dear?" he countered, beginning to pace along the rooftop. He paused and turned his gaze back to her. "Do you feel they have paid for those?"

She hesitated, then shook her head. "The LN never did anything to me. *You* were the one who killed my father, and it was Arhyen's sister who abducted him and cut him open, not the London Network."

"Do you still not understand?" he questioned, whirling on her with sudden intensity. "All of these things began with the London Network, and it will all end with them too. I never should have been created."

"Then I suppose you feel the same about me?" she questioned, trying to remain calm. "Will you kill me too?"

He chuckled, seeming to slip back into his normally relaxed demeanor. "No, my dear. I have grown . . . attached to your existence, just as I've grown attached to mine. It never should have happened. I was never supposed to care if I lived or died." He tilted his head again as he observed her. "I was never supposed to care if *you* lived or died."

She took a step toward him. "Then let us both live. Let us leave this place before something horrible happens."

"Horrible things have already happened," he muttered, turning his gaze toward the distant sound of shouting. He turned back to her. "London will not be quiet after this. The balance of power has shifted. I'm here to ensure that those in power previously never rise to the top again."

Liliana glanced about nervously, wondering just how Hamlet intended to prevent that rise.

Observing her, he laughed. "Alright, alright. The very least I can do is sate your curiosity." Signaling for her to follow, he turned away and began walking across the roof.

She stared at his back in shock. Was he really going to divulge his final plan when she was there to stop it? Perhaps he really had gone mad, but she wasn't about to pass up the opportunity.

She carefully watched her steps as Hamlet led her across the roof. She briefly wondered if she could just push him off the edge, but knew, just like with the poison, she wouldn't be able to go through with it. He was leading her toward what appeared to be a large metal box mounted in the center of the roof, though it was too dark for her to make out any details. He stopped in front of it, then waited for her to join him.

"This is my grand finale," he explained, gesturing toward the box with a black gloved hand as she approached him.

She gazed at the contraption. It was about her height, and twice as wide. She had no idea how he'd gotten it onto the roof, but she supposed it didn't matter. It was here now.

"What does it do?" she asked.

Hamlet patted the top of the contraption lovingly. "The center of the cube contains a large amount of one of your father's synthetic emotions. Below the vestibule are several sets of pipes leading down into different rooms of the palace."

"So it's the same thing you did earlier?" she asked, confused. "I saw the people in the streets affected by the emotions. It was frightening, but the effects wore off."

He chuckled. "Yes, their emotions wore off because the Advector Serum was used. This contraption contains a far different serum."

She glanced at the cube again. "Wh-what does it do?" she stammered.

"This serum is permanent," he explained. "It will fill all within and surrounding the palace with sadness and despair. They will be forced to feel the suffering they have caused for others, and there will be no escape."

Liliana took a step back. Could it be possible? Could inhaling a chemical cause someone to sink into despair *forever*?

"They'll go mad," she gasped. "They'll kill themselves."

Her attention was drawn toward the front of the palace as those wielding torches began to attack the guards. Screams of rage and grunts of pain rang out across the cool night air.

She sensed Hamlet's presence at her back. "Yes they will," he replied coldly. "They *all* will."

Something dangled beside her shoulder. She looked away from the fighting men to see a cylindrical, black mask-like object hanging from multiple black straps. Hamlet extended his gloved hand, offering her the object.

"Only you and I will be safe," he explained.

She stared at the contraption, then glanced back at Hamlet and gasped. He had removed his mask to reveal his scarred face. Rivulets of skin ran down his cheeks and chin, narrowly missing his nose and mouth. His eyes were also whole, though scars dripped down either side of his brows.

He lifted another object like the one he offered her, and demonstrated by placing the cylinder over his mouth and nose before pulling the straps back over his head.

He once again offered her the other mask. "You'll want to put that on, unless you'd like to kill yourself with all the others."

She stared up at him in disbelief. "You knew I'd come," she accused, her voice barely above a whisper. "You knew I'd come here to stop you, perhaps to *kill* you. I don't understand why you would bring me a mask."

He leaned his tall frame forward until they were face-to-face. She gulped at the close view of his scars, and couldn't help her sympathy. Tears threatened her eyes.

"You are a victim of their actions," he explained, ignoring her tears as they began to spill over. "I do not wish to harm the victims."

"Well you're about to!" she pointed down to the men fighting below, unable to hear her over their own shouts.

She stepped back out of reach, then swatted at something in front of her face. She continued trying to clear her vision, then realized in her panic that it was snowing. As a sudden thought dawned, she glanced at the synthetic emotion contraption over her shoulder, wondering if the snow would eventually freeze the liquids within.

"Do you think I've not prepared for all circumstances?" Hamlet asked, as if reading her mind. He once again extended the mask to her.

She took another step back. "What if I refuse to wear the mask? What then? Will you sacrifice me along with all the others?"

"I could force the mask upon you," he suggested.

She took another step back, searching her mind for another option. She took one more step, and the heel of her boot hit the edge of the roof, slick with falling snow. She nearly stumbled, but managed to right herself.

Hamlet tilted his scarred face in thought, looking frightening and foreign in his odd mask.

She glanced behind her at the three-story fall. She could survive a lot of damage, but could she survive *that*?

"If you jump," he began calmly, "then I most surely will follow through with my plan."

She glanced down again, then back to him. "Not if you promise not to." She raised a brow at him. "You are a man of your word, are you not?"

"What do you mean?" he demanded.

She shifted her other foot back so that both heels were balancing on the edge of the roof. "I mean that if I jump, I don't think you're fast enough to save me. So either promise me right now that you won't use that contraption, or we'll see if I can survive a three-story fall."

He began to move forward, but she stopped him by moving one heel further off the edge of the roof.

"One more step, and I'll jump," she threatened.

The snow was beginning to pick up, blurring him slightly in her vision.

"Liliana," he began. "Though I do not want to see you die, you will not stop me. If you must go down with the others, then so be it. I'd rather see you broken on the ground, than mad with despair."

Her breath hitched. It wasn't going to work. If she fell, it wouldn't stop him.

"Liliana!" a voice called from below.

Her heart fell in her chest. She'd know that voice anywhere. She turned to pick him out of the crowd below, but her heel caught and she stumbled. Suddenly she was airborne, falling away from the roof into the cool night.

"No!" Arhyen screamed. He'd been such a fool to call out to her. He'd just been caught off guard when he recognized her shape on the rooftop. He'd reacted without thinking.

He watched in horror as she stumbled, then fell. His heart stopped for several seconds, then a dark shape darted from above and caught her. They hung in mid-motion for a brief moment before dropping to the ground.

Arhyen's hands flexed around the bars of the gates as he glanced toward the guards. The angry mob had caught up with him as he'd been circling the perimeter, attempting to find an unguarded way into the palace. He was glad for them now, as they created the distraction he needed to scale the tall gates unhindered. He quickly scurried over, then dropped to the grassy ground on the other side, nearly slipping on the ice forming there. He peered toward the palace, barely able to see through the ever-thickening falling snow, but he thought he saw a lump on the ground near the palace wall.

"There was someone on the roof!" one of the guards shouted from behind him.

Arhyen raced forward on the slippery grass. They must have seen Liliana fall. He had to reach her first.

He skidded to a halt near the shape on the ground. Sweat dripped down his temples and he was barely able to breathe. He crouched beside Liliana's still form. Whoever had fallen with her was nowhere to be seen.

Unsure if she was alive or dead, he gathered her into his arms. He chose to believe she was alive, for it was the only way he could go on. Her body was frighteningly limp, and her clothes damp. He wondered for a moment why she was wet, then it clicked. She must have swam up to the palace, then snuck in through the back, though he had no idea how she'd made it up on the roof. There was no time to think about it now, she'd at least given him a way to escape.

With her secured in his arms, he raced the best he could across the palace grounds toward the lake. Several of the guards fighting off the angry mob branched away from the group, shouting about getting up on the roof.

He glanced over his shoulder to see if they pursued him, but the heavy snowfall obscured them from his sight. Hopefully it would hide his escape.

Reaching the back of the grounds, he groaned, looking up at another tall fence barring him from the waterway. As a normal man, he would never make it over the fence carrying her, and was unsure if he could now, but he had to try.

He hoisted her up, draping her over his shoulder. He clamped one arm around her thighs, securing them against his chest, then he began to climb.

The climb seemed to take forever, and the snow made the bars slick beneath his bare hands. He feared the guards would be upon them any moment, and there would be no way to explain why Liliana had fallen from the roof, nor how he'd so quickly scaled the gates to rescue her.

By the time he reached the top, he was shaking from the cold and exertion. It was all he could do to lower himself on the other side, clinging tightly to Liliana as he loosened his grip on the fence and tumbled to the snowy bank below. He wrapped his body around Liliana to absorb the impact of the fall, losing his breath as they hit.

"Get up," a familiar voice hissed.

Still holding on tight to Liliana's limp body, Arhyen opened his eyes, thinking perhaps he had died climbing the gates, and now was stuck in an odd dream as his soul left his body.

"Get up," Ephraim hissed again, crouching down to grab hold of Arhyen's free arm. He helped him to his feet, then took Liliana from him as she began to slip from his shoulder.

"How did you find us?" Arhyen asked blearily as he stumbled after Ephraim.

"I arrived just as the mob approached the palace," he explained. He bumped Liliana more securely over his shoulder, hurrying toward a nearby boat. "I didn't see you, nor did I see Liliana, so I figured I may as well use the distraction to get into the palace and stop Hamlet. I paddled across the lake, and had just reached the shore when I saw you drop from the gate."

They reached the small rowboat Ephraim had pulled up onto the sandy bank. At Ephraim's instruction, Arhyen pushed the boat into the water, then held it steady as Ephraim gently lowered Liliana into the vessel. Ephraim climbed in next, taking up an oar as Arhyen pushed the boat further into the water and hopped in. He took up the second oar and began to paddle in rhythm with Ephraim. The long lake spanned far away from the palace. If they could reach the far side unseen, they could easily disappear into the night. Hopefully the guards would be too busy inspecting the roof and fending off the mob to notice their departure.

Paddling furiously, Arhyen shivered, unable to look down at Liliana lying motionlessly beside him. Part of him knew she must be dead after such a fall, but he simply could not accept it. He'd seen someone else fall with her, presumably Hamlet, yet he'd disappeared. If he could survive the fall, then so could Liliana.

They paddled onward as the snow continued to drift around them, and began to stick on the damp surfaces of the boat, twinkling in the moonlight. The mixture of snow and soft light made everything glisten, once again causing Arhyen to feel as if he was in some sort of dream.

When it was clear they were not followed, he put down his oar and moved forward to kneel beside Liliana. He gathered her limp body in his arms.

"Is she . . . " Ephraim trailed off, remaining seated.

"No," Arhyen snapped, though he knew it was a lie.

He held Liliana close, listening for her breath, her heartbeat, or any other sign that she still lived. Nothing presented itself.

Tears streamed down his face. This was all his fault.

He'd tried to make her leave the city. He'd tried to make her go home. He should have known all along to keep her by his side where she belonged.

He kissed her cold, still face over and over, dripping tears onto her pale skin. Snow began to gather in her red hair, and he wiped it away. His thoughts distantly echoed that she'd lost her black cap somewhere, though the thought was irrelevant. He held her tight as the world seemed to crumble around him.

His mind flitted to vengeance, then to Hamlet's plan, but none of it seemed to matter. It didn't matter what he did if Liliana would no longer be by his side. London could burn to the ground for all he cared. He'd gladly burn it himself.

Suddenly her body convulsed in his arms. At first he thought it must be some sort of trick, or that the boat had lurched in the water, then her body convulsed again.

Unsure what was happening, he lowered her back to the floor of the boat. She lurched again, then her chest rose as she sucked in a gasping breath.

Ephraim cursed behind him in shock, though Arhyen barely heard. With another ragged breath, Liliana's eyes fluttered open.

He wasn't sure if he was crying or laughing as he leaned forward and pushed her damp, icy hair out of her face. He wanted to pull her back into his arms, but feared moving her. Her eyes seemed out of focus as she blinked up at the falling snow.

She scooted back until she could get her arms beneath her, then slowly sat up. She glanced around in confusion, her eyes finally settling on Arhyen's tear streaked face.

"What happened?" she murmured. "Where's Hamlet?"

He was briefly overcome with rage at the mention of Hamlet, but managed to stuff it back down. "I saw him fall with you." Fresh tears began to stream down his face. "You were dead, Liliana. Your heart was not beating."

She shook her head. "That's not possible. I remember him falling with me. I remember . . . " she trailed off. "He hit the ground first and shielded me as we rolled across the grass. Then everything went black, and now I'm here. Did he set off the device?"

"What device?" Ephraim asked while Arhyen attempted to compose himself.

She shook her head and gazed off into the distance. After a few silent seconds she explained, "He claimed to have discovered a way to make my father's synthetic emotions permanent. Honestly, I think he might have been infected by them at some point too, though I don't know if it was intentional. He wanted to fill everyone in and around the palace with despair to make them pay for their crimes. It didn't seem to matter to Hamlet that many innocents would be sacrificed."

The lost tone in Liliana's voice broke Arhyen's heart. It was as if she'd just learned that her entire worldview was wrong. She had hoped to find good within Hamlet, and he had let her down . . . but then, why had he saved her?

"The guards were all rushing to check the roof when I picked you up and ran," he explained. "Hamlet's device may very well be in their hands now, if he hasn't killed them all."

Liliana startled back into seeming awareness. "Do you think they'll understand what it is? What will they do with it?"

He didn't know how to answer her. If the Queen and her Guard really were in control of the London Network, they'd either lock the technology away, or use it for their own purposes. Either way, they weren't likely to move forward with any plans until Hamlet had been caught.

Finally, he shook his head. "Unfortunately that cannot be our primary concern. If Hamlet's plan has indeed been thwarted, at least for tonight, the LN *might* not come after us right away, but I wouldn't count on it. The deal was that my efforts would lead to his capture, or his death. I do not believe either will happen tonight."

The boat bumped against the end of the lake.

"So what do we do now?" she asked.

Ephraim sighed. "We wait for the sun to rise, and see if there's anything left of London, or our lives, to save."

CHAPTER 11

The next morning found them in Ephraim's home. Liliana had never been there, and had never thought she would. As much as he delved into other people's business, Ephraim was an exceedingly private person. The second story apartment was more cozy than she'd expected, with overstuffed furniture in much better shape than Arhyen's threadbare sofa. His kitchen was small and tidy, and his cupboards nearly bare, hinting that he was rarely home. The decor in the small home was sparse, save several sets of shelves overflowing with books and a large desk draped with a map of the city. Through one door near the front was the bathroom, and through another next to the kitchen was the bedroom where Ephraim had retired. Arhyen and Liliana had snuggled up for the rest of the night on the sofa, though neither had slept much.

As morning dawned, Liliana sat on the sofa next to Arhyen, peering through the curtained window as she sipped her tea. It was beginning to grow light outside, but the streets were eerily quiet.

She jumped as a loud crash sounded somewhere outside. Though most of the looters had retired, a few were still out taking advantage of the missing Watch and Queen's Guard. She shook her head, wondering how many innocent men and women had perished like Ephraim's colleagues at Watch Headquarters.

She peered down into her half empty cup of tea, then jumped again when she turned to find Arhyen watching her intently.

"How are you feeling?" he asked.

She shrugged, unsure of how to answer his question. Physically, she felt fine, but she also felt like bees were buzzing in her head. Her thoughts were anxious and scattered. She hated sitting still waiting for something to happen.

"Do you think Hamlet will try to get back to the palace roof?" she questioned instead of answering.

He shrugged, then rubbed his tired eyes. "If he hasn't already." He glanced at Ephraim's bedroom door, as if expecting him to soon emerge.

"Do you think the LN will try to capture him when he does?" she pressed.

He sighed and slumped back against the sofa cushions. "They've been trying to capture him for weeks. I don't see why they'd have any more luck now than before."

"Do you think we should leave London?" she blurted.

She'd been thinking about it ever since she woke up in the boat. If she'd never come to London, Arhyen wouldn't be involved in any of this, but it was too late to take it back. Her only hope now was that they could escape the chaos together.

Clearly exhausted, he raised an eyebrow at her. "Do *you*?"

She looked down at her lap. Her heart was racing and she wasn't sure why. "I don't like the idea of giving up, but I can't help but feel I'm making things worse. I've had multiple opportunities to stop Hamlet, and I've failed every time."

"You stopped him from using his device," he answered, placing a hand gently on her shoulder, "even if you did it by falling off a roof."

She smiled softly at him. "I didn't do it on purpose, you know."

Still leaning back against the sofa cushions, he removed his hand from her shoulder and held out his arm. She set her teacup on an end table, then snuggled against him, laying her head on his warm chest.

"You know I nearly died myself when I saw you fall," he muttered against her hair, curling his arm around her.

"Well apparently I actually did die," she chuckled. Suddenly serious, she craned her neck to look up at him. "What would you have done if I had?"

"Honestly, I don't know," he answered. "If you would have asked me that yesterday, I would have said that I'd avenge you, but after nearly experiencing your demise, I'm not sure. All I could feel was great loss in that moment. I couldn't consider what was happening in the city, or what Hamlet was doing. Suddenly none of it mattered."

She snuggled back against his chest, taking comfort. "We both should stop nearly dying. I don't think our hearts can handle it any longer."

He wrapped his arm a little tighter around her to place his hand on top of hers, sending a little thrill through her body. It was like the adrenaline she felt right before falling off Buckingham Palace, but without the fear. She was never really afraid when she was with him.

Her head shifted as he sighed. "I'm beginning to think the only way for us to accomplish that is to leave London altogether. Not this minute I mean, but after all of this is over. If we both survive, perhaps we can travel the world. Coming so close to death has made me realize that there's a lot I still want to see."

She raised her head to look at him again. "Truly?" she asked, her heart suddenly filled with hope. "I've always wanted to visit Egypt."

He raised an eyebrow at her. "To explore hidden tombs like in your adventure novels?"

She laughed and rested her head back upon his chest. "If you must know, yes." Suddenly feeling somber, she added, "but first, we need to make sure you won't suffer the same fate as Christoph."

"Christoph?" he questioned.

"The Captain of the Watch," she reminded him.

"Ah," was his only reply.

The bedroom door creaked and Ephraim emerged, interrupting their conversation. He'd dressed in fresh clothes and combed his blond hair. "Now who's ready to see what remains of the city?" he asked, renewed excitement twinkling in his eyes.

Liliana sat up, worry twisting her gut. She glanced at Arhyen, ready to argue with him should he insist she stay behind.

Instead, he turned to her and asked, "Are you ready?"

Her eyes wide, she nodded. "You're not going to try to make me stay here?"

He chuckled and shook his head, then peered at her through strands of his shaggy brown hair. "I've learned my lesson. The only place I want you, is right by my side."

"Oh for heaven's sake," Ephraim muttered, heading toward the door to retrieve his coat.

Liliana grinned at his back, then turned her smile to Arhyen as he stood and offered her his hand. She took it, suddenly feeling ready to face whatever awaited them outside.

❧

ARHYEN'S BOOTS CRUNCHED THROUGH THE SNOW coating the street. His sturdy black coat flapped against the back of his knees, keeping time with the crunches. Liliana matched his pace, with Ephraim sandwiching her in the middle. The black clad trio appeared quite the sight, their clothes and affirmative gait befitting their mood.

Arhyen eyed other courageous souls who had emerged onto the streets, seemingly as fed up with hiding as he was. No one tried to speak to them. The few other citizens brave enough to leave their homes were preoccupied with staring at broken glass storefronts, scorched remains of ruined buildings, and corpses scattered amongst the rubble. Arhyen suspected most were killed by fires or angry mobs, but some must have been killed by the synthetic emotions. The emotions themselves might not kill, but people infected with rage could be dangerous to others, and those infected with despair were dangerous to themselves. The snow had covered many, leaving only white fluffy lumps to mark their temporary graves.

"What if there's no one there?" Liliana muttered, referring to their agreed upon destination, the facility where Arhyen had been held when recovering from his injuries. Although Hamlet had hinted that it had been attacked, some of the London Network might still remain.

He was nervous about confronting the LN, but needed to be sure they knew he and his associates were the reason Hamlet's attack on the palace did not go as planned, even if they'd thwarted him on accident. Of course, Hamlet might have gone back to finish the job, unbeknownst to them, and the London Network would kill him on sight, but it was a risk he had to take.

He didn't see any other choice.

Liliana cleared her throat, still waiting for an answer.

"If no one is there, then we'll return to the palace," he explained.

"If there's anything left of it," Ephraim added.

He sighed and walked around a body only partially covered in snow. He kept his eyes averted, looking anywhere but down. He'd seen dead bodies before, but not like this. This was . . . he had no words for it. All he knew was that he wanted Hamlet to pay for what he'd done. He could only hope that Liliana had come to the same conclusion.

Soon they reached their destination. At least, what was left of it. Where once stood a nondescript brick building, now was only rubble, covered in snow. He stepped forward to examine the remains. While he'd been mostly confined to a single room, he knew that room was underground. The small glimpses he'd caught outside the room hinted at an expansive underground compound. Of course, Hamlet had known that too. He might have destroyed everything and everyone within.

It was still worth a shot.

Ephraim and Liliana followed him silently, occasionally kicking bricks out of the way or moving melted beams in search of a way down. He watched as Liliana effortlessly lifted a heavy charred piece of metal, revealing concrete stairs.

She was about to walk down when Ephraim grabbed her arm. "The heat from the fire and explosions has likely weakened the concrete," he explained. "Those stairs may crumble beneath our feet."

She stepped away from the stairs, then warily glanced at the rubble near her boots. What remained of the floor they now stood on also served as the roof the basement, but Arhyen thought the sudden worry unnecessary. The fact that none of it had crumbled along with the rest of the building meant it was heavily reinforced. There could still be plenty of evidence below them. Evidence the London Network would return to collect if any of their operatives still lived.

"I'll go down first," Arhyen decided. "It's worth the risk."

Casting a wary eye on the stairs, Ephraim took a step back. "I'll keep watch up here."

Arhyen met Liliana's waiting gaze.

"I'm coming with you," she stated.

"I wouldn't dream of stopping you," he smiled gently, then led the way down the stairs. Each step felt solid beneath his feet, giving no signs of crumbling. Feeling more sure of himself, he picked up speed as he descended into the dark abyss, with Liliana following closely behind.

He could barely see two fingers in front of his nose by the time he reached the bottom, and wished he had thought to bring a lantern. With only the small amount of light streaming in from the stairs to see by, it would be impossible to find anything of use.

He felt Liliana's presence by his side as she reached the landing. "I'm afraid we'll have to rely on your superior night vision," he whispered. "Can you see anything?"

"A bit," she whispered. "It's a total mess down here. Everything must have been thrown around from the impact of the explosion."

She took a few steps forward, then suddenly turned and hurried back to his side. "There also seems to be a man down here," she added, her voice shrill with surprise.

"Didn't mean to startle you," a voice sounded from the darkness. "I was just searching for some medicine."

"What's going on down there!" Ephraim called from the top of the stairs.

Arhyen moved in front of Liliana, though he could not see exactly where the man was in the darkness. "What kind of medicine?" he asked, ignoring Ephraim's question.

"It's bright blue," the man explained, his voice accompanied by the sound of shifting objects. Suddenly he revealed a small lantern, illuminating his face. "I fear my supply has been damaged," he continued, "and this seemed a fitting place to look for more."

Footsteps on the stairs behind them signaled Ephraim's approach. Arhyen shifted, making room.

Ephraim reached the bottom and gave Arhyen a quizzical look before turning his attention to the man with the lantern. "C-Christoph?" he stammered. "But you're . . . "

"Dead?" the man replied absentmindedly, still paying them little attention as he shuffled through the debris.

"Wait, Christoph?" Arhyen questioned, recognizing the name. "You mean the Captain of the Watch who framed us for murder?"

Christoph finally turned his full attention to them. "Ephraim?" he questioned in surprise. "What on earth are you doing here?"

Ephraim gawked at Christoph. "I could ask you the

same question, given you're supposed to be dead. I saw your body. What is this, necromancy?"

Christoph sighed and sat his lantern on the concrete floor. "I see I'm going to have to explain myself," he began. "You all may as well come in." He shifted his gaze to Arhyen. "I assume you are Mr. Croft?"

He nodded, utterly confused to be speaking with a dead man.

Ephraim took a single step into the room, crossing his arms as he glared at Christoph. "Explain," he demanded. "Are you one of the London Network's experimentations?"

"I suppose you could say that," he replied. "The corpse you saw was actually an automaton, made in my image. The London Network sent it to replace me when I went to them for help. You see, I have a terminal illness. But they were not the first I turned to for aid. I first went to-"

"My sister, Hazel," Arhyen finished for him. "And in exchange, you covered up her nefarious activities, and framed us for murder. We know all that."

Christoph raised both bushy eyebrows in surprise. "My, how astute of you. I suppose I'll just skip to the parts you do not know. It eventually became clear to me that Hazel had no intention of offering me a cure. I had framed a friend for murder." His apologetic gaze settled solely on Ephraim. "And I was no closer to saving my own life. I knew that Hazel Croft at one point had worked with the London Network, so I went to them for help."

"But how did you find them?" Liliana interrupted.

Christoph turned his gaze to her as if just noticing her presence. "My lady, I was the Captain of the Watch, a valuable ally. As soon as I started looking, they found me." He turned his gaze back to Ephraim. "They offered me a way out. I would allow an automaton to take my place running the Watch, and they would give me a cure. They came through, but now all of my medicine has been destroyed."

"The blue liquid all over your home," Liliana gasped. "We thought it was something that had been forced upon you, and in the struggle, spilled everywhere."

Christoph shook his head. "I do not know what happened to it, but it was something I took willingly, something I need to continue taking in order to survive."

Arhyen watched as Ephraim stroked his chin in thought. "Was this automaton living in your home, the one that looked like you?"

Christoff nodded. "He was. It was part of my agreement with the London Network. I was to go into hiding while the automaton took over my life. I had been prepared to leave with a large amount of my medicine the very next day, but when I returned home it was all destroyed, and the automaton was gone. Then my confession was all over the papers."

"I see," Ephraim replied. He turned to Arhyen and Liliana. "I believe Hamlet is to blame for all this. As a favor to *you*," his gaze landed on Liliana, "he went to Christoph's home to extort a confession. What he found was an automaton and a large amount of medicine. He must have somehow convinced the automaton to confess Christoph's crimes, then he destroyed the rest of the medicine, leaving the mess we found."

"Who on earth is Hamlet?" Christoph interrupted.

Ephraim glared at him. "He's the one terrorizing all of London, or didn't your LN friends bother to tell you that?"

"They tell me very little," he sighed. "I'm of no value now that I'm supposed to be dead."

Liliana cocked her head. "What I don't understand is why the automaton died in his jail cell if the London Network wanted him alive."

Arhyen pursed his lips in thought, then replied, "I don't think they were the ones who killed him. There is a secret passage leading out of the jail. That's how Hazel got to me. Anyone could have snuck in. The fact that there were no signs of foul play leads me to believe it was Hamlet, disposing of the evidence once Christoph's confession had been made."

"Well that's one mystery solved," Ephraim muttered. He turned his glare back to Christoph. "Do you know where the leaders of the LN can be found now?"

Christoph sighed, slumping against a nearby wall. "I imagine they're regrouping at Buckingham Palace, if any are still left alive. If you find them, can you tell them I need more medicine before I can disappear forever?"

"Wait," Liliana interrupted before Ephriam could reply with what was likely a scathing remark. "So you need a constant supply of this medicine to stay well?"

Christoph nodded. "My illness is incurable. It eats away at my body. This medicine is quite miraculous. If you took a straight dose, you could even heal a fresh injury in minutes. The medicine heals the damage caused by my illness, but it does not cure the affliction."

Arhyen watched as Liliana's face lit up. She turned toward him. "If that truly is the case, then you should be fine. If your infection is gone, and your incisions healed, then you should not need any more of the medicine to sustain you. Your afflictions were not caused by a permanent disease."

He widened his eyes in sudden realization. He'd been so preoccupied unraveling the mystery of Christoph, he hadn't even been thinking about his own encounter with the vibrant blue liquid. Grinning, he pulled her into a hug, which she happily returned.

"Well they're sweet," he heard Christoph comment to Ephraim.

Ephraim grumbled something under his breath, then marched back toward the stairs. Halfway there, he turned to meet Arhyen's gaze. "Unless you believe we'll actually find useful evidence in this mess, I'd advise we depart." He glared at Christoph again. "I would wish you luck, but I would not mean it."

Christoph smiled sadly. "I suppose I deserve that."

Ephraim began to ascend the stairs, then stopped. He moved the front flap of his coat, then reached into his waistcoat pocket, withdrawing the bright blue vial. He tossed it in Christoph's direction.

Christoph leapt to his feet and caught it, then stared down at the vial in awe.

"Do something meaningful with your remaining time," Ephraim muttered, then finished his journey up the stairs.

While Arhyen hadn't appreciated being framed for murder, he felt sympathy for Christoph's plight, and gave him a final nod. The medicine might prolong his life, but his disease would inevitably return.

Christoph raised his eyes from the vial to meet Arhyen's waiting gaze. He gestured toward him with the vial. "This is enough to heal my entire body within minutes. The results won't last forever, but it's a start."

"It can really heal you that quickly?" Liliana asked. "That's absolutely fascinating."

Christoph nodded, then lovingly secured the vial within his waistcoat pocket. "I'd tell you more if I could. All I know is it's nothing short of a miracle." He turned his gaze back to Arhyen, then with his free hand, gestured toward the open air where Ephraim had disappeared. "Take care of him, will you? I wouldn't want another friend to let him down like I have."

Arhyen nodded. "Thank you for your help, I suppose, though I wouldn't get your hopes up about acquiring more medicine to last you once the vial is gone. The London Network has been severely weakened. I doubt they'll be in a giving mood."

Christoph nodded, a somber expression on his face. "I suppose you're right. Perhaps I was never meant to cheat death in the first place."

Arhyen nodded again, then gestured for Liliana to ascend the stairs ahead of him. He would have liked to agree with Christoph's final statement, but he was beginning to make a regular habit out of cheating death, so he couldn't, in good conscience, throw any stones.

CHAPTER 12

Arhyen followed Liliana up the stairs of the compound, leaving Christoph behind. Once they were back in the dreary light of the gray day, Ephraim made no further comment on his previous friend and employer. Arhyen suspected he was relieved to see the man alive, even after his massive betrayal. Not that he'd likely be alive for long . . .

With a final glance at the ruined compound, he sucked in a cold breath of air, prepared to venture back to Buckingham Palace. He found himself wishing he could talk to Wakefield about all he had learned. Had Wakefield actually been honest with him about the London Network's intentions? It seemed so. He couldn't help but wonder if those who worked for the London Network were truly his enemies. While he didn't agree with keeping possible cures for diseases from the public, he wasn't sure if they'd committed as many crimes as he thought. They had left Christoph alive after all, and had even provided him with medicine as part of their bargain, when they simply could have killed and replaced him with their automaton.

Although, they *had* created Hamlet, a ruthless killing machine. If they paid for nothing else, they should at least pay for that. He shook his head as they began walking, their boots crunching across the snow. Perhaps the London Network was already paying for their crimes. Hamlet was making them pay tenfold.

Liliana took his hand and gave it a squeeze, drawing him out of his thoughts. At first he thought she was simply being affectionate, then he noticed a woman trudging through the snow toward them. It was his mother.

"It's about time I found you," she groaned, continuing her approach. "My old bones are not fairing well in this cold."

He took in her gray hair, pulled back into a tight neat bun, and her black dress in pristine condition. The shawl around her shoulders looked new too. Not only had she clearly not been out in the chaos of the previous night, but she apparently had found someone new to take care of her. There was always someone, wasn't there? You could get far in London if you were willing to sacrifice your morals for someone else's.

"What do you want?" he sighed as she reached them. "I thought you were arrested."

She raised a thin gray brow at him. "And how did you know about that?"

"Ephraim and I tried to find you," Liliana explained to her. "A child described those who apprehended you. At first we thought the Watch responsible, but when you were not in the jail, we deduced you'd been taken by the Queen's Guard."

"That I was," she beamed. "They came asking after

my son, and whether he had any friends I could point them to."

Ah, Arhyen thought. Wakefield had omitted that they'd tracked down his mother. He supposed he couldn't blame him, given he was desperate to find Hamlet. He realized too that his failure to cooperate with Wakefield initially had likely contributed to the current state of affairs with his mother.

"And are you here to take us to Wakefield?" he asked.

She blinked at him in surprise. "W-why yes. How did you know?"

"Explain," Ephraim interrupted.

Arhyen turned to him. "Wakefield was the man with whom I negotiated my release, the same one we met in the street when one of Hamlet's henchmen was killed. He had initially wished me to divulge any of my associates who might know the location of Hamlet. When I refused, he went looking for my mother, a logical choice since we share the same surname. She then found a way to make herself useful, rising from prisoner to employee."

Catherine nodded. "That about sums it up. Now if you'll come with me, Captain Wakefield is waiting."

Liliana began to walk forward, but he held out an arm to stop her. "Waiting to speak with us, or to kill us?"

She rolled her eyes. "Do you truly believe I'd lead you to your death?"

He simply stared at her. She'd practically done just that with Hazel.

She pursed her thin lips, then sighed. "Wakefield bade me tell you they apprehended Hamlet's device from Buckingham Palace, whatever that means. He assumes that since it wasn't set off, someone must have interfered with Hamlet's plan. If it was you, Wakefield is in your debt."

"*Whatever that means?*" he questioned, then slowly smiled. "So you've been promoted to messenger then, nothing more. They're wise to not share unnecessary information with you."

"Don't look so smug," she growled. "At least I'm alive, and I've been offered protection, which is more than you were willing to do for your own mother."

He sighed. In his mother's eyes, everything would always be his fault. There was no point in arguing. "Take us to Wakefield," he said finally.

Nodding as if satisfied, she turned and began walking back over the footprints she'd made in the snow.

After casting wary looks at each other, Ephraim, Liliana, and Arhyen followed.

❧

LILIANA RECOGNIZED THE AREA CATHERINE LED THEM toward. It was a lot closer than Buckingham Palace. The tall white gates of White Heights loomed before them, heavily guarded by members of the Queen's Guard along with several men in normal clothing. Most of the men were battered and bruised, with soot staining their uniforms and visible skin.

"Oh what I wouldn't give to never enter this neighborhood again," Arhyen muttered beside her.

Liliana agreed. They'd last entered White Heights to spy on Clayton Blackwood, and had nearly been captured in the process.

Catherine glanced back at them, but continued walking. She'd been uncharacteristically silent during their journey, and Arhyen had seemed all too happy to do the same.

Catherine approached the nearest guards, who both seemed to recognize her. They looked Arhyen, Ephraim, and Liliana up and down, then gestured for them to follow Catherine through the gates.

Liliana kept a close eye on the guards as they passed, not trusting the seeming truce. "Where do you think she's leading us?" she whispered.

"No idea," Arhyen muttered.

They followed an already well-trod path through the snow, walking gingerly on the slippery surface. Several of the guards left their posts to follow behind them, while Catherine continued to lead the way. Liliana noticed that a few homes showed signs of attack from the previous night's chaos, but the damage was far less than the rest of the city had suffered. She wasn't sure if it was mere coincidence, or if Hamlet had avoided the neighborhood since the wealthy homes of White Heights were usually well protected.

They walked onward until Catherine stopped before the guarded gates to a massive mansion, its tall walls matching the uniform white of the entire neighborhood. The building looked stark and cold in the surrounding snow.

The gate guards, dressed in the gold buttoned coats and the tall hats of the Queen's Guard, did not move to admit them to the premises. Instead, the gates let out a hiss of steam and swung inward of their own accord.

"Are we sure about this?" Ephraim muttered under his breath.

Arhyen shook his head, but replied, "Do you have any better ideas?"

Liliana watched as Ephraim shook his head, then

marched forward dutifully. The guards behind them cleared their throats, and Liliana and Arhyen jumped to follow.

Liliana sucked in an unsteady breath, then let it out to fog the air. She felt more uneasy now than she had all morning, like they were walking into a trap. A few guards marched behind them as they approached the mansion's massive double doors, where four more guards were posted. It seemed like there was more security here than there had been at Buckingham Palace. Really, she was surprised there were still this many guards left alive.

Arriving at the double doors, one guard on each side opened them, revealing Wakefield waiting just inside. His dark blue uniform, bedecked with numerous medals, was rumpled and covered in soot, though his face was clean and his gray hair appeared freshly combed. He stepped back, arcing his palm outward, inviting them to come inside.

As they entered, Catherine stepped forward from the group, clearly expecting orders or some form of acknowledgement from Wakefield.

The doors behind them shut with a loud thud, followed by the sound of locks clicking. Liliana tensed at the sound, her nervous energy increasing.

Wakefield absentmindedly waved Catherine off. She scowled, then crossed her arms and waited as Wakefield spared a nod for both Ephraim and Liliana, then turned to Arhyen.

"I appreciate you coming," he stated politely. "Queen Victoria would like a word with you."

Liliana turned to Arhyen to see if he was as shocked as she.

His eyes practically bugged out of his head. "You must be kidding me," he balked.

Wakefield narrowed his gaze. "I assure you, I'm not much of a . . . kidder. After I expressed my belief that you had something to do with Hamlet not using the device he'd mounted on the roof of the palace, the Queen asked that you be found, and brought to her at once." He eyed Ephraim and Liliana in turn. "Along with your associates," he added. "Now if you'll please follow me." He began to turn away.

"My son saved the Queen's life," Catherine interrupted, "surely he deserves a great reward."

Wakefield halted. Turning toward Catherine, his gaze narrowed further. "Saved? Hardly. The Queen was not at the palace last night," he assured. "We would never be foolish enough to leave her so vulnerable once the attacks began."

Liliana used the distraction to take in the rest of the room. The tiles beneath their feet were a beautiful shade of ivory, with veins of peach and gold. The wall paper echoed the colors beautifully, accented by the gold and white furniture gracing the empty spaces of wall not taken up by doors. Just judging by the entryway, the estate seemed fit for a queen. Could she really be in the same building as them?

She turned back to see Catherine's face pink with rage, but she did not interrupt further as Wakefield began to lead them toward one of the nearby doors.

Left with little choice, they followed.

Arhyen gave Liliana a grimace as they walked, clearly stating, *I should never have brought you here*.

A guard moved to open the door where Wakefield had led them. One by one, they filed into a long hallway bedecked with ornate rugs and paintings in gold frames. The hallway ended with an open door, leading into a large room dominated by a massive, dark wood table.

Liliana's eyes darted around as they entered to room. At one end of the massive table sat a somewhat plump elderly woman in an ornately patterned blue brocade dress. Though the lines on her face hinted she was likely in her seventies, her erect posture and keen glint in her eyes made her seem far younger. At her back stood two more uniformed guards, along with several more posted at the large windows lining one side of the room, and two at either door. Glancing at the guards' rifles and rapiers, Liliana suddenly felt small and vulnerable.

As if on cue, one of the guards at the Queen's back stepped away to stand near the window.

Wakefield moved forward to replace him, then held his arm out in a sweeping gesture."May I present to you, her most gracious majesty, Empress of India, Queen Victoria."

The seated woman smiled as Ephraim, Arhyen, and all of the guards bowed.

Liliana watched wide-eyed, then practically fell to the floor, mimicking their behavior before it was too late.

"Please rise," the Queen said kindly. "Now is not the time for formalities."

Blushing, Liliana rose with everyone else, then looked to the Queen for further instruction.

Victoria's gaze settled for a moment on her, making her gulp, then next moved to Ephraim, then Arhyen. "Which of you is Mr. Croft?"

Arhyen stepped forward and bowed, making Liliana wish she'd at some point studied the proper protocol for meeting a queen. The behavior seemed to come naturally to Arhyen.

"You have my thanks," Victoria continued, her eyes lingering on Arhyen's dirty clothes. "While I was not in the palace during the attacks, you have undoubtedly saved countless lives."

Arhyen mumbled, "I was only doing what was right," then bowed again, deeper than before, appearing more naive with the protocol than it first seemed.

The Queen simply smiled at his behavior, then gestured to the other guard who'd remained at her back, a man in his mid to late fifties, with graying black hair and a neatly trimmed beard. The man stepped around the table, then approached Arhyen. As he reached him, Liliana noticed a rolled piece of parchment in his hand. He extended it to Arhyen, then returned to his post behind the Queen.

With a nod of encouragement from Victoria, Arhyen unrolled the parchment.

Liliana leaned a bit to her right, attempting to see around his shoulder to the parchment he now read, but before she could, he lowered the parchment to his side, unaware of her effort to see.

"A pardon?" he questioned.

Victoria nodded. "For *all* of your crimes. Captain Wakefield researched you fully, it seems you've had a minor, yet *busy* career."

Liliana was quite sure she could hear Arhyen gulp.

"It will all be forgiven," she continued, "if you do your queen one last favor."

Arhyen cleared his throat. "And what might that favor be?" he asked boldly.

Wakefield bristled at his tone, but did not speak.

Victoria smiled a little wider. "I would like you to go into the city and start an uprising. I want you to give Codename Hamlet exactly what he desires."

If Liliana thought she was dreaming before, she was quite sure of it now.

"Why?" Arhyen blurted.

Wakefield stepped forward, his hand on his pistol. "How dare you-"

The Queen cut him off with the raise of her hand. "It's quite alright, Captain. I will answer the question. The lad needs to know just what he'll be attempting to achieve." She turned her gaze back to Arhyen. "I'm going to skip the formalities and assume you know about some of the scientific discoveries in the possession of the London Network. I will also assume you know that Hamlet hopes to expose our organization, after fatally weakening it. If he has his way, the people of London will learn just what has been kept from them. Not only that, but they'll learn that their homes were destroyed, their loved ones' lives lost, all for science. It is the latter I hope to avoid. I would like you to lead a revolt, demanding better treatment of London's lower class. You will demand food for the hungry, shelter for the homeless, and better wages for the working man. You will storm the palace, and after a short negotiation, I will give in to your demands."

Rolling her eyes at Arhyen, she raised her hand again. "Before you once again so rudely ask *why,* I implore you to think about what I have said."

Liliana watched Arhyen as he seemed to mull things over. She hoped he understood what the Queen was asking, because she surely did not.

After a moment, he nodded. "If enough witnesses see you giving in to my demands, the people will begin to believe that that's what all of this violence was about. They will believe their fellow citizens rebelled in hopes of gaining them better treatment. They surely will not blame their peers for violence in the name of equality, and their ruler will appear magnanimous for giving in to such demands. London will be rebuilt, and no one will ever know just what Hamlet was fighting for."

The Queen nodded. "I see my suspicions were correct, and I was wise in choosing you. Do you agree to my terms?"

Arhyen seemed to think for a moment. "So, you want me to lead a revolt and lie to my fellow citizens, and I will be pardoned of all crimes." He glanced back at Ephraim and Liliana. "I assume my associates will be pardoned as well."

Liliana's back stiffened as the Queen's gaze landed on her. "Yes," she replied, "and your *associates* as well."

"You have a deal," Arhyen agreed.

A shiver ran down Liliana's spine. Was this truly the right choice? She turned toward Arhyen, who looked back and offered her a subtle nod, but she still couldn't help but feel he'd just signed their lives away.

❧

TOGETHER, ARHYEN, EPHRAIM, LILIANA, AND Catherine left the Queen's temporary abode in White Heights. Liliana cast a wary eye on Catherine, unsure why she was joining them, but she hadn't asked questions. She had been more than ready to get out of the mansion and away from the Queen's eerie gaze.

Once they were beyond the white gates and the guard's view, Arhyen's hand landed on her arm, stopping her. Ephraim stopped beside them, then both men turned toward Catherine.

"We require a moment alone," Arhyen stated, gazing cooly at his mother.

Catherine's face reddened, then her breath fogged the

air as she huffed, "We're supposed to be organizing a mob, not chatting in the street."

Arhyen simply stared at her until she backed down and skulked away, muttering under her breath. He was really quite good at that icy stare. Once Catherine was out of earshot, he turned back toward Liliana.

"The Queen knows what you are," he hissed, "just as she knows what I am."

The nervous feeling that had been twisting in her gut tightened its grip. "I noticed her looking at me strangely, but how could you tell?"

"The guards," Ephraim explained, keeping his voice low. "Those who followed us in, and those already waiting inside. They all watched you and Arhyen, but barely spared a glance for me. When we were meeting with the Queen, they were all concentrated near the two of you, as if ready to leap into action should you try anything. They know you're an automaton, and they know Arhyen is now nearly one himself."

Arhyen nodded, sweeping his shaggy hair out of his eyes with his palm. "She will not keep her deal, there's no way. Not after everything that Hamlet has done. She might let me slide by since I started out human, but you," his gaze lingered on her sadly, "you started life as an automaton, just like Hamlet. Wakefield told me that most automatons are remanufactured after a few years to keep them from malfunctioning. I believe the type of malfunction he was referring to is . . . Hamlet."

Her pulse raced. It was one thing to fear *malfunctioning* and going mad, quite another to have those fears voiced by another. "Do you truly think I'll become just like Hamlet?" she croaked.

His jaw fell. "N-no!" he stammered. "Not at all. I'm simply implying that the Queen might think that, and I do not believe she'll risk another automaton following in Hamlet's footsteps. She may pardon our crimes publicly, but that won't stop her from making us disappear afterward."

Ephraim glanced back at Catherine waiting across the street by a lone streetlamp, then nodded. "Agreed. So what do we do now? If we don't incite a rebellion soon, I've no doubt Victoria's guards will track us down."

Arhyen frowned, glanced worriedly at Liliana, then back to Ephraim. He seemed to be mulling something over. Suddenly, his expression hardened. "I think we should expose the London Network once and for all, even if it means we must leave the city for good."

"Arhyen," Liliana began, but he shook his head.

"Perhaps that's what we should have done from the start," he continued. "Say our peace and be done with it. If they still want the city after all has been exposed, they can have it."

Could they really do that? Could they somehow expose the London Network, and live long enough to escape London altogether? Part of her wanted to try, but there was still one problem. "Hamlet is still out there, and he will not give up his plans. If we expose the LN and leave the city, there may be no one left to stop him."

Rather than outwardly sharing in her fears, Ephraim calmly stroked his chin in thought. "The Queen didn't seem terribly worried about him," he commented finally. "She spoke as if he was still a threat, but if he was, she would already know her *plan* was futile."

Arhyen tilted his head. "You know, you're right. She mentioned nothing of him in regards to her plan, and her guards were all in uniform. If she still felt the need to hide from Hamlet, she would not have made her hiding place as obvious as it was. Perhaps they managed to capture him."

Liliana shook her head in disbelief. He was impossible to capture. They'd been trying for weeks.

"I doubt they'd keep him alive," Ephraim added, "which would mean that threat has been eliminated entirely."

She felt sick. She knew Hamlet deserved punishment for his crimes, but she simply could not picture him dying. "S-so he's gone?" she questioned, wanting absolute confirmation. "She spoke of him like he was still alive," she added, unable to cope with the thought.

The last she'd seen of Hamlet was when they fell off the roof of Buckingham Palace, but according to Arhyen, he'd disappeared. If the guards had captured him, it was sometime after she had been rescued by Arhyen.

"I don't believe we can make any assumptions based solely on the Queen speaking as if he were alive," Ephraim began. "Either he's dead, or the Queen's plan is actually just a ruse to lure him into a trap. That would make just as much sense. The blatant display of guards in White Heights could have been the first trap, but seeing it for what it was, Hamlet stayed away. He might be an evil killing machine, but he is no fool."

Arhyen sighed, "So either we're the Queen's backup plan for luring out Hamlet, or he's dead, and we're simply her scapegoat so she won't be blamed for the chaos. Once again, we are left entirely in the dark."

Still cursing under her breath, Catherine crunched up in the snow behind them, effectively ending their conversation. "Can we get on with this now?" she questioned sourly.

Arhyen met Liliana's gaze, then nodded. "Let's go."

Numb and confused, Liliana felt almost paralyzed,

buried deep in thought. She felt Arhyen grip her arm gently, guiding her along as they continued away from White Heights. If this was all a trap for Hamlet, then executing the Queen's plan would not serve them. What good would it do to hold up their end of the bargain if Queen Victoria knew she was an automaton? Automatons were supposed to have owners. They were supposed to blindly obey. She was a product of the exact sciences the London Network wanted to keep hidden. She would never be allowed to live her life freely again.

She glanced worriedly at Arhyen as they walked, but he seemed buried deep in thoughts of his own. He was as much a product of science now as she. Leave the city to its fate, he had suggested, and that is where her thoughts now lingered.

She found herself more than ready to do just that.

❧

ARHYEN WATCHED HIS MOTHER'S BACK AS THEY trudged through the snow toward Market Street. More and more, London's citizens were slowly emerging from hiding as the chaos was seemingly over. Some searched through the snowy rubble of ruined buildings, perhaps hoping to find their loved ones still alive. Mothers wept for their lost children, and lost children wandered the streets like tiny zombies in search of their parents. These people had lost their homes and their livelihoods, right as cruel winter hit. Perhaps those who died in the initial chaos were lucky. Their deaths were quick. Many more would starve or freeze if they weren't offered aid.

Eyes still on his mother's back, he suddenly hated her more than he ever had. Would she have even cared if he'd been among the dead? Would she have searched the rubble along with the other mothers?

He doubted it, which is why he felt little guilt over what he was about to do.

As soon as they passed by those congregated in the streets, he looked to Ephraim, making sure he had his friend's attention.

Ephraim searched his face for a moment, then nodded. There was no way for him to know Arhyen's exact plan, but he would back him up without hesitation.

As they left behind the last cluster of people and were clear of witnesses, or any who might intervene, he grabbed his mother's arm and half pushed, half carried her toward a nearby shop.

She let out a surprised yip, then began a fruitless struggle. Being just as small as Liliana, with no automaton strength to back up her protests left her dangling in Arhyen's grip as he carried her past the shop's broken front windows, and in through the wooden door hanging on a single hinge. Once inside, he hurried Catherine across the shop's wooden floor, hoping to find a room deeper within the establishment before she came to her senses and started screaming. She continued to struggle against him, bruising his shins with the back of her boots.

"Unhand me!" she grunted, kicking her feet back toward his shins again.

He ignored her cries and the screaming pain in his shins, moving her along so fast he nearly tripped a time or two. There had to be a storeroom area here somewhere, hopefully with its door intact. He sighed in relief when he actually found one, filled with toppled crates already combed over by looters. He shoved her inside, then joined her, followed by Liliana and Ephraim.

"What do you think you're doing!" Catherine shrieked, glaring daggers at him.

Arhyen retreated to the door and closed it behind them. "Mother," he began patiently. "I'm sorry for the rough treatment, but truly, this is for your own good."

"You're going to get us all killed," she spat. "All you have to do is carry out your orders and you'll be safe. Lead some silly rebellion, then we can all get on with our lives."

Ignoring his mother, he turned to Ephraim and Liliana. "I must ask, if my plan works, will you both be prepared to leave the city?"

After a moment's thought, Liliana nodded. "As long as I leave with you."

Ephraim chuckled and shook his head. "I have no intention of leaving, but don't let that spoil your plan. I do love a good caper."

Though he didn't like Ephraim's answer, he nodded. He knew if it came down to life or death, Ephraim would leave with them. The man was stubborn, but rarely foolish.

He turned back to his mother. Her gray hair had come loose from her bun, and her shawl had fallen from her shoulders. She looked small and pathetic.

He crossed his arms, unwilling to feel sympathy for her. "It's better for you if you don't know our plan," he explained, "so we'll be leaving you here. Please trust that I'm doing this for your own good."

"Like you care anything about my own good!" she hissed, wiping at her bright red, and tear-rimmed eyes.

His face drooped. Sympathy after all. She might be cruel and selfish, but after all she'd done, she was still his mother, and he was about to say goodbye to her for the final time.

She continued to huff, looking a bit ridiculous, and he smiled. "You'll do well to remain here until everything calms down. You won't see me again after this. I'm going to live my life free of the burdens you've placed upon me in the past. I hope that in the end, you can find your happiness." He glanced at Liliana and broadened his smile. "And I hope you can be glad that I found mine."

Catherine blinked at him. Her jaw slowly opened and closed, but no words came out.

"I'm going to barricade the door once we leave," he continued, turning back to her. "I'm sure you'll manage to escape eventually."

Ire flashed through her eyes, then she made a lunge for the door, only to be intercepted by Liliana. She tried to dart around her, but Arhyen moved to bar her way.

Wordlessly, Ephraim opened the door and left the room, stepping into the hall with Liliana close behind. Stepping backward, Arhyen followed them, keeping a close eye on his mother.

"You'll never truly leave this city," she growled. "You're no better than me."

His smile didn't falter. He'd long since given up on proving anything to her, but just this once, he'd be absolutely sure to prove her wrong.

"Goodbye, mother," he muttered.

She glared at him as he shut the door in her face.

Given there was no lock, he leaned hard against the door to secure her as she started screaming and pounding to get out. "Grab that desk," he instructed Ephraim, pointing to the heavy, roll top desk topped with a destroyed cash drawer.

Ephraim obeyed, pushing the desk across the wood floor. Arhyen stepped back as they slid the desk against the door.

Catching on, Liliana effortlessly lifted a heavy, overstuffed chair and carted it across the room, shoring it up against the desk to strengthen the barricade. It would take Catherine at least a few hours to find her way out, and if they were lucky, a few hours was all they would need.

He looked to Ephraim and Liliana, awaiting his further instruction.

Focusing his gaze on Liliana, he asked, "Do you still have our leverage?"

Looking unsure, she patted her coat pocket, then nodded. "You were there when I lost the poison, but the blue vial is still intact."

Arhyen grinned. "Excellent, now it's time to lead that angry mob to the Queen."

His eyes nearly twinkling with excitement, Ephraim nodded his agreement.

Liliana furrowed her brow. "But I thought we *weren't* going along with the Queen's plan."

"We're not," he explained. "But we'll need an audience before we reveal everything the London Network has been hiding."

CHAPTER 13

Arhyen ran as fast as his legs would carry him across the slippery cobblestone street. The snow had begun to melt, leaving him to navigate the treacherous slop that remained. They'd decided to split up in hopes of gathering a large group of people quickly. Ephraim took Market Street since they were already there, and he couldn't travel as quickly as Arhyen and Liliana. Liliana took Tailor Street, and Arhyen took the bordering residential area. Once they'd gathered their groups, they would march past the old abandoned mansions of the once wealthy district, then on toward the palace.

It would be risky doing their *demonstration* there, but he wanted the Queen to believe everything was going as planned until the last minute. He could only hope his mother wouldn't escape prematurely to ruin this one last chance to set things right.

He reached his destination, the largest, lower class residential area in the city. If he was going to find anyone to march on to the palace with him, he would find them here.

He slowed his run as he scanned the street. The small homes seemed undamaged, as if the chaos had not touched down here. He supposed it made sense. Hamlet had targeted the areas where people would be out and about during the day. The same areas that housed government buildings.

Though a few people had emerged from their homes to peer about warily, they didn't exactly seem like the types to join an angry mob. He didn't want to enlist those who had small children to look after, nor anyone too old to keep up. Mobs could be just as dangerous to their members as their opposition, and he would regret anyone getting trampled.

He paused for a moment to listen, wishing he had Liliana's exceptional hearing. This neighborhood wasn't going to work out. He needed a more active area of the city.

"Psst," someone hissed from behind him.

He whirled around, then saw a masked face peering out from behind a nearby bush. At first he thought it was Hamlet, then he realized the figure was too small, and had long, blonde hair peeking out from beneath his or her black cap.

He took a curious step forward, then hesitated. He was not sure if Hamlet currently considered him an enemy or ally, so he could not predict how one of his henchmen would react.

Still crouched, the figure waved him over from behind the bush, revealing a female form in men's black clothing.

With a wary glance over his shoulder, he gave in and trotted toward the masked woman.

She glanced around, then stood as he reached her. "I saw you yesterday," she explained, her voice soft and breathy.

He thought back, wondering what she was talking about. His mind flashed on yesterday when Hamlet offered to drink poison for Liliana. He'd had henchmen with him. She must have been one of them.

"And?" he pressed, anxious to get on with his quest. He glanced around again, but no one seemed to be watching them.

He heard a nervous inhale of breath behind her mask. "Do you know where Hamlet is?" she whispered. "None of us have been able to find him."

Curious, especially after the Queen's lack of concern over his whereabouts. "Who is *us*?" he asked.

She took a step closer to him. "Those who no longer wish to be oppressed," she replied cryptically. "None have seen Hamlet since he went to the palace last night. We fear the worst."

His body tensed with the urge to step back, but he resisted. He sighed, his mind briefly racing for an explanation, but he had no time for this. "I haven't seen him either, and I'd like to know just as much as you what he's planning now. Unfortunately, I have other business to attend to." He turned to leave.

"Please don't go!" she gasped, reaching out for him. "I don't know what I'm supposed to do next. I have no one to guide me, nowhere to go."

Guide her? He paused, then looked her up and down. Was she perhaps an automaton stolen away from her *owner*? It would make sense. Who else would join Hamlet willingly?

"Can you remove the mask?" he asked.

The girl simply stared at him through the realistic eyeholes of her porcelain facade.

"Listen," he began patiently. "If you're looking for something to do, I need to gather a large group of people in a short amount of time. Can you help me?"

She seemed to think for a moment, then nodded. "There are many of us. We split up to search for Hamlet, but have plans to reconvene."

He clenched and unclenched his fists anxiously. This might actually work. "You'll all have to remove the masks," he explained. "You'll need to appear like normal citizens, and reveal your true identity to no one. "

She hesitated for a moment, then slowly lifted her gloved hands to remove her mask. Her face was lovely and young, with the perfect smooth skin common amongst female automatons. Yet, that was where the similarities ended. Her gaze was not the blank, emotionless gaze of an artificial construct. She was scared.

"What did Hamlet do to you?" he asked, his mind jumping to the synthetic emotions. "Did he have you inhale any sort of vapor."

She shook her head, then looked down at her feet. "I was supposed to be destroyed. Remade into a new automaton for my owner. I had become . . . defective. Hamlet rescued me."

He stared at her in sudden realization. Just as Wakefield had hinted, automatons were remade every few years to avoid . . . defects. Were the defects he referred to human emotions? Could any of them develop true emotions if given enough time?

"What is your name?" he asked, mulling things over.

She smiled broadly at the question, raising her hand to push staticky strands of blonde hair from her face.

"Marie. That is the name I chose after Hamlet rescued me."

He pursed his lips in thought. Fear still lingered in her eyes behind her smile. He couldn't imagine all the poor girl had been through under Hamlet's care. He didn't like involving such a seemingly sweet girl in his plan, but since she was an automaton, she could handle her own physically. Plus, she'd be safer on *his* team than on Hamlet's.

"Marie," he began, "I need you to gather the rest of your associates, and meet me where you saw me yesterday with the red haired girl."

Her smile broadened. "You mean Ms. Breckinridge? Hamlet said she's one of us. We can trust her."

He fought to hide his cringe. Of course she knew what Liliana was. Hamlet had probably told them *all*.

"Yes, you can trust her," he assured. "She will be waiting for us at that location."

She nodded. "Then we will see you soon. We will not let you down." With that, she turned around and ran off, impossibly lithe and graceful.

He watched her run until she disappeared down the icy street. While he wasn't surprised Hamlet had recruited automatons as his henchmen, he was worried. They'd been so easily coerced into destroying the city. What other atrocities could they be capable of if they fell into the wrong hands?

Shaking his head, he turned to leave the neighborhood and search for Liliana. If Marie could gather enough automatons, they might not need to recruit as many humans as he'd thought.

LILIANA STARED AT WHAT WAS LEFT OF THE

storefront. She'd seen this shop before. It was where Arhyen had seen Hamlet's mask in the front window. Now, the front window was shattered. Costumes were strewn about the floor, trampled by looters looking for more expensive items like jewelry. Masks littered the area, some cracked underfoot, and others dangling from the few displays yet standing, but she did not see one like Hamlet's.

Her gaze moved to a similar mask, hanging from a bent metal display. She wondered what she would have done, had her creator dripped acid on her face, forcing her to wear a mask for the rest of her life. Would she have ended up just like Hamlet? Perhaps he truly was evil for all the harm he'd caused, but she couldn't entirely fault him for it. Maybe if she was human she'd think differently, but she wasn't human, and she knew she could have just as easily been subjected to the same treatment as Hamlet.

"No luck?" a voice asked from far behind her.

She jumped, then turned to see Arhyen approaching. She let out a sigh of relief. She wanted to run toward him, throw herself into his arms, run her fingers through his perpetually messy hair . . .

"The city seems so quiet today," she observed, calmly. "I fear I have failed in my task."

She had come to Tailor Street with the intention of gathering people to march on the palace, but the few folks she'd seen had been frightened, glancing around the street warily as they hurried to wherever they were going. She hadn't even bothered trying to speak with them.

Arhyen closed the distance between them, his black coat flapping in the cool wind. Somehow knowing her secret desires, he pulled her into his arms. "Don't worry, Liliana. I think I found enough people to help. If

Ephraim can come through with some from the Market District, I'm sure we'll be able to gather more on our way to the palace."

Now she felt like even more of a failure. She'd be the only one who did not contribute. Still, Arhyen's warm body felt nice against hers, and she couldn't help but relax. "Where are the people you found to join us?" she asked.

"They'll meet us soon," he said cryptically. "Don't worry."

With her arms around his waist, she laid her cheek on his chest. Normally she'd feel uncomfortable sharing an embrace in public, but at that moment, she needed it. "What if this doesn't work?" she breathed.

He lowered his face to kiss her cheek, then replied, "It doesn't matter. We'll be leaving the city regardless. I just want one last chance to set things right . . . as right as they can be at this point, anyway. Then we can leave the city behind with no regrets."

"And what is *right*?" she asked, still nestled in his arms. "For the life of me, I cannot seem to decide. Is the London Network right? Is Hamlet? What about *us*?"

"None of us are right," he replied bitterly, "or all of us. Rightness is in the eye of the beholder, if you will. We're all doing what we think is right."

She sighed. It was all so complicated. "Where will we go when we leave the city?"

He pulled back so he could see her face, his hands lingering around her waist. "I believe you mentioned something about Egypt?"

She gasped and met his gaze. "Truly? Do you think we could actually go to Egypt? I know we've discussed it beforc, but I never really thought it possible. It's such a long ways away."

His arms around her shifted as he shrugged. "We'll have to work a bit along the way, but we'll get there. I hope you're not opposed to continuing your training as a thief's apprentice."

She grinned up at him. "As long as we only steal from people who deserve it."

He chuckled. "Then Egypt it is. We'll live by our own version of what we think is right, and not give a damn about anyone else's."

"And we'll explore hidden tombs and go on adventures?" she pressed, feeling a small thrill of excitement trickling through her.

He let his fingers drop from her waist, then took her hand to begin walking. "Whatever you like."

"And if I go mad like Hamlet?" she blurted out the fear she'd been holding inside.

He stopped walking, then turned to study her expression. "Are you kidding?"

She shook her head, unable to meet his gaze. "No. It's a possibility. If his existence has caused him to go somewhat mad, it could happen to me too."

He gently brushed his finger beneath her chin, lifting her gaze to his. "Then I'll go mad right along with you," he whispered. "Where you go, I go, Liliana."

She swallowed the lump in her throat. While theoretically she'd known he would stay by her side, a part of her had needed to hear it.

He gave her another kiss, then took her hand again to tug her forward.

"You know," he began as they jogged along.

Sensing humor in his tone, she turned her gaze up to his face. "Yes?" she prompted.

He grinned. "Well I was just thinking, most would say

we've both already gone entirely mad, so we really shouldn't worry."

She laughed. "You know, I think you're right. We've both been entirely mad from the start."

They both laughed as they continued running, a testament to any onlookers that they were both completely, utterly, stark raving mad. Liliana didn't mind the occasional stares. The only opinion that mattered to her, was that of the man running right by her side.

❧

TOGETHER, ARHYEN AND LILIANA REACHED THE dilapidated mansions of the mostly abandoned wealthy district. Arhyen's palms sweated with nerves, despite the iciness of the air. Would Marie show up with all of Hamlet's henchmen, or would they be entirely dependent on those gathered by Ephraim? That was, if he managed to gather anyone at all. Who knew forming an angry mob could be so difficult?

"I don't see Ephraim anywhere," Liliana muttered, peering one way down the street, then the other.

He tapped her shoulder to get her attention, and they both began walking. They were still a few blocks away from where they'd met with Hamlet.

As they walked, Arhyen grew increasingly hopeful of gathering a crowd. So *this* was where everyone in the city had run off to. Families gathered together, prying boards off the windows and doors of the long-since abandoned mansions. The buildings were run down, but hopefully structurally sound since they were built with expensive materials. Truly, the ornate buildings had gone to waste for far too long, and he was glad to think they might see some use.

"Why would they all come here?" Liliana whispered, glancing at those waiting to enter the buildings.

"It makes sense," he replied. "The Watch regularly clears out the vagrants from this area, so it's been entirely deserted for years. This is likely one of the few neighborhoods entirely unaffected by yesterday's attacks. It's a fitting place for those who have lost their homes, especially now that the remaining officers of the Watch have better things to do than clear out the destitute."

He followed her gaze as she watched a woman portioning out a hunk of bread to several small children sitting in the icy grass near the edge of the cobblestone street.

"Perhaps we shouldn't have come here," Liliana observed somberly. "I don't want to bring these people further troubles."

He nodded in agreement. "Let us find Ephraim, and those I have hopefully recruited. If any others want to join us, it will be their choice . . . " he trailed off. Looking past Liliana, his jaw dropped.

"Is that-" Liliana began, equally stunned.

Just coming into view further down the street was Ephraim, marching along in front of a massive mob of men and women in varying degrees of dress. Some were clearly destitute, wearing little more than rags, while others wore more expensive frock coats and top hats. Arhyen and Liliana waited in stunned silence as the crowd approached.

Ephraim raised a hand to bring the crowd to a halt, then raised a blond eyebrow first at Arhyen, then at Liliana. "I see you both have failed?" he asked pompously.

The crowd began to mutter behind Ephraim, so he motioned them forward. "It's unwise to keep a mob waiting," he muttered. "I'd like to avoid dissension amongst our ranks. You can both explain your failures later."

Arhyen and Liliana quickly shuffled forward, leading the crowd in the direction of the palace.

"*How?*" Arhyen balked, moving to walk at Ephraim's side. "How did you gather so many?"

Leaning close to his shoulder, Ephraim explained, "I started with locating a few of the remaining officers of the Watch, then we divided and conquered." He gave Arhyen another skeptical look, silently commenting on his lack of followers.

"Mine are still coming," his hissed, eager to defend himself. "Hopefully," he added.

Just then, a young blonde girl came trotting along the side of the crowd. "Mr. Croft!" she chirped, raising her hand.

She caught up with them and started marching alongside Liliana, who stared at her speculatively.

"Were you able to gather everyone?" Arhyen shouted to her over the murmur of the crowd.

She nodded excitedly, causing him to glance back. The crowd slowly expanded as black dressed figures filtered into its ranks. If Ephraim's mob only knew they were being joined by those responsible for yesterday's attacks . . . he shook his head and turned his attention forward.

"*You're* Miss Liliana," he heard Marie whisper.

"Do I know you?" Liliana replied.

He wasn't able to hear Marie's reply over the crowd, but caught Liliana asking, "Hamlet? Is he still alive?"

He turned to see Marie shrug and shake her head, indicating she did not know.

Liliana turned her worried gaze to him, but he could only shrug and shake his head as Marie had. He doubted

Hamlet was dead. He would not be surprised if he came out of hiding at the absolute worst time, when they had the Queen and the majority of the guard all gathered to provide an audience to their angry mob.

In fact, that was probably *exactly* when Hamlet would come out of hiding to have his long-awaited finale. Arhyen could only hope the distraction would prove large enough to cover their escape.

CHAPTER 14

Arhyen gripped Liliana's hand, perhaps too tightly, unsure if his plan would manifest. No matter what, he wanted to be by her side until the end. Any of them could be killed in such a daring show of bravado, or at the very least, imprisoned. He knew it would be difficult to escape the city after what they were about to do, let alone find transport across the countryside after the previous day's events.

Yet, he saw no other choice. He could not let the London Network blame the terror of the day before on its own citizens. The London Network had created Hamlet. If anyone was responsible for all the deaths, it was the Queen herself.

He glanced back to see Marie marching along with the crowd. He spotted several other faces that were likely other automatons. Though none wore masks, they all wore black like Marie. Fortunately, the humans in the mob did not seem to notice, as they were entirely swept up in their march on the palace. They wanted to demand better pay, more human rights, all of the things the

Queen had instructed Arhyen to demand. They might even get them, if not in the exact way they hoped.

London was already teetering on the edge of revolution. Once he revealed the truth to its citizens, the word would spread. Nothing could go back to the way it was before. Change was inevitable. Whether that change would be in the favor of the lower class was yet to be seen.

The palace came into view, shrouded by gray mist on such a moist day. It looked like a haunted castle from a distance, with its surrounding street lamps creating eerie orbs that seemed to be floating in the fog.

"Remember what we discussed?" he whispered, leaning close to Liliana's shoulder.

She nodded, then gave his hand a squeeze. "I'm ready."

As they continued to near, the Queen's Guard came into view, along with the Queen herself. She awaited them on a raised dais, surrounded by her armed men. He thought it quite brazen for her to be out in the open with the threat of Hamlet still lurking, unless he wasn't. Perhaps Hamlet truly was dead, which would explain the Queen's apparent lack of concern. So much for a distraction to cover their escape.

The crowd began to murmur their surprise at seeing the Queen waiting for them. Upon closer observation, Arhyen spotted abundant guards posted on the palace roof, and positioned around the green they were approaching. He scanned the nearest buildings and noted guards atop and around most of them. He swallowed the lump in his throat. If they made it all the way to the Queen, they would be completely surrounded. He'd hoped for a head-on type of confrontation, where they could escape back the way they'd come. With how the guards were set up, as soon as he disobeyed the Queen's orders, they would likely all be killed.

"Are you sure about this?" Ephraim muttered.

"Yes," Liliana answered for him, "It will be alright."

Arhyen met her gaze, wondering at her assurances. Surely she saw the guards spread out across the area, just waiting to execute them should they step out of line.

She nodded to him. "We'll go ahead with things as planned. *Together*."

He wanted to tell her to run. He wanted to shove her away with everything he had, if only to keep her from the execution that surely awaited them.

"Together," he breathed, then gave her hand a squeeze before dropping it.

They reached the first row of guards before the Queen, who sat regally on her dais, heavily flanked by more of her men. Her ornately embroidered coat shielded her comfortably from the cold. The mob, some of whom were freezing in their rags, went silent behind Arhyen.

"Good citizens of London," the Queen announced, raising her voice for all to hear, "I await your demands."

A few shouts rang out across the crowd, drowning each other out to make their words unclear.

Arhyen nodded his acknowledgement to the Queen, then turned toward the mob. He couldn't quite believe what he was about to do.

"Good people," he began, raising his voice to be heard above the murmurs of the crowd, "you have marched here today to demand better wages, better treatment, and the respect you deserve! Your queen is willing to accept your terms, but it is all for naught." He paused as the murmuring grew louder. He resisted the urge to glance back at the Queen, expecting her interruption any second.

He cleared his throat. "Your beloved queen would like to mislead you!" he continued. "All of this chaos, this destruction, was the result of the Queen's direct actions. She has chosen to play god, and has hidden valuable information from you. She owes you for your lost homes, and the lost lives of your loved ones, and not only the recent losses. The atrocities inflicted upon you span years!"

"Clearly he speaks mistruths!" the Queen shouted from behind him, just like he'd been expecting. This was where things would get ugly. "Guards!" she screeched, "arrest that man!"

He whirled around before the guards could charge, holding up his hands as if to ward off their attack. They hesitated, likely expecting him to either run, or offer violence.

"If I'm already to be deemed a liar," he blurted, darting his gaze past the guards to the Queen, "then surely there is no harm in allowing me to finish. Truly, the only plausible reason for my arrest in this moment is to prevent me from sharing my proof."

The mob behind him shouted their agreement, for now, still on his side. If his proof did not convince them, he would become their victim.

Surrounded by a protective wall of guards, Queen Victoria sneered down at him. "You have no proof."

"Oh?" he questioned, making sure his voice was loud enough to carry across the crowd. "Then why have me arrested?"

Her sneer melted into a haughty smile. "Go ahead with your little plan. The people of London are no fools.

They'll soon see your claims as false, and you will be given the imprisonment you deserve, *thief.*"

It was only then that he noticed Wakefield standing at the Queen's back, amongst the other guards. He met Arhyen's gaze for a single heartbeat, then nodded.

Confused, Arhyen nodded in return, then turned to face the crowd. With a flourish, he withdrew his dagger. He knew many of the guards would see what he was doing, but from this angle, the Queen would not. Hopefully he could finish before she had him dragged away.

"Watch," he instructed those nearest to him.

Those in the first row of the mob leaned in, observing him curiously.

He lifted his sleeve, then ran his dagger across his forearm, drawing a bright red line of blood. Some in the crowd gasped, and a few of the guards muttered in confusion. He held his arm out for those nearest to examine, to prove the wound was real. After a few in the crowd nodded in verification, he extended his uninjured arm to Liliana, trading the dagger for the blue vial she'd withdrawn from her pocket. Taking the vial, he held it up to show the crowd, then popped the stopper off with his thumb. With a silent prayer, he drank the blue liquid, hoping it would work as fast as Wakefield and Christoph had claimed. Allegedly such a large dose could heal a shallow wound within minutes.

He held his bloody arm out to the crowd for several quiet moments. His stomach churned with anxiety. Even this might not be enough proof, if it even worked at all, but at least he had their attention. In a grandiose gesture, he swiped the blood on his arm away with his other sleeve, revealing the miraculously healed skin beneath.

"The wound is gone!" one of the nearest men in the

crowd gasped. Excited murmurs erupted deeper within the crowd.

"But that doesn't explain why we were attacked!" someone else shouted.

He glanced to Liliana, ready for her to launch into her explanation of what the blue liquid was and where it had come from, but she simply shook her head and smiled.

Suddenly, something sailed through the air from the direction of the nearest rooftops. With a light thud, Hamlet landed beside Liliana, crouching to absorb the impact of his impossibly far jump. As he straightened, Arhyen realized he no longer wore his mask. The pale, scarred skin of his face was visible, absorbing the murky sunlight.

"Twas I who attacked you!" he announced to the crowd. "Twas I, a creation of your beloved queen." He rolled his hand in the air, then ducked into a bow in the Queen's direction.

Arhyen glanced at Victoria, awaiting her next move. Her face was flushed, her breathing seemed heavy. If she ordered her men to attack Hamlet now, she'd never be able to refute the claims against her. The mob was too large to be imprisoned. Many would escape to spread word to the rest of the city.

The crowd was silent for several heartbeats, then Marie stepped forward. "He speaks the truth!" She crouched, then sprung into the air and landed beside Hamlet, showcasing her inhuman grace. "I too am a manmade creation. One that was made to wait on your every need. You were told I could not think, could not feel. But I *can* feel. For that, I was set to be *destroyed*."

The crowd erupted in gasps and murmurs, slowly shuffling away from Hamlet and Marie. They were afraid of them, ready to turn on them for what they'd done. It couldn't happen this way. They needed to blame the Queen.

Liliana stepped forward, looking small and harmless, even in her black attire. "I too, am nothing but a synthetic creation," she announced meekly. "I did not take part in the attacks. In fact, I worked to stop them. Still, I understand why they did it."

The crowd murmured again, then went silent, hanging on her every word. The Queen seemed unable to decide what to do. Perhaps she was hoping Liliana would still follow through with the plan they'd agreed upon, hoping to save her own hide.

"What would you do, if you were told you were incapable of love, yet you felt it?" she questioned, her voice growing in strength. "What would you do, if you were told you weren't a real person, but for the life of you, you could feel everything a real person feels? When we," she glanced at Marie and Hamlet, "begin to feel the emotions you all take for granted every single day, we are destroyed and remade, by order of the Queen. A woman," she began, then cleared her throat to speak more loudly, "A woman who has the formula to heal all that ails you!" She gestured toward Arhyen and his healed arm. "A woman who has the ability to provide synthetic organs to replace your failing ones! She can cure any illness, yet she does not. She hoards her secrets and divulges them only to the wealthy elite. You may blame those who attacked you for taking lives, and you would be entirely right to do so, but you should just as equally blame the woman who has been taking your lives for years! Forcing you to live in poverty, and die needlessly!"

"Hear hear!" several members of the crowd shouted.

"You should blame the woman responsible for the government that has created such unfair wages and conditions, while the wealthy live on your backs!" Liliana continued, surprising Arhyen with her observations. "Blame those who force you to live in squalor, working your lives away for every meal, while those with wealth buy automatons as slaves so they'll never have to work a day in their lives! Every death that has occurred is not the fault of London's citizens. The guilty party stands before us!" She gestured back to the Queen and her guards.

"Here here!" more in the crowd shouted.

Finally the Queen had had enough. She stood and bellowed, "Arrest them all! This is treason!"

The guards began to march forward.

Arhyen took Liliana's hand, prepared to fight his way out and protect her at the same time.

"Halt!" someone shouted from behind the Queen. The guards stopped moving.

Arhyen turned to see Wakefield step forward on the Queen's dais. "Everything the girl said is true!" he announced. "*Everything*," he reiterated. "You have all been lied to! The Queen could have provided you all with advanced medical care, yet she did not. Many have died to protect her secrets. You live in poverty, in part, to fund research from which you will never benefit."

The guards began to mutter amongst themselves. It was obvious that they were not all privy to the information being bandied about.

"I am your queen!" Victoria shouted. "Now arrest them, unless you would all like to be executed for treason!"

Some of the guards began to swarm forward once more, but others hesitated. Arhyen heard someone question, "Could the Queen have saved my wife? She died of pneumonia last winter." Someone else in the crowd muttered about their lost son. Then more and more began to question.

The guards still obeying the Queen reached Liliana and Arhyen, but Ephraim stepped between them, then surprisingly, Marie stepped in front of him.

Hamlet, nearly forgotten during Liliana's speech, turned toward the crowd. "Protect these good people!" he shouted. "It was never our aim to harm *them*." It became clear who he was speaking to as those in the crowd wearing all black separated themselves to face the guards.

Arhyen stared at Hamlet in disbelief. "This was your plan all along. You sent Marie to find me, and you let everyone believe you were dead until just the right moment. You let us gather everyone together so that you might have your finale."

Hamlet snickered, crinkling his scarred face in a way that made Arhyen's stomach turn. "The Queen's men *killed* me," he explained. "Or so she was told. Your good friend Captain Wakefield made a deal with me to save many lives. He really is a good man."

"Arhyen," Liliana hissed, tugging on his hand. "I think it's time."

While the majority of the crowd was pushing forward, some were branching off from the back and running toward the city.

"They will spread the word," Hamlet observed. "And my people will protect the crowd to see this through. It's time for you to go."

Liliana released his hand, then threw herself into Hamlet's arms, wrapping him in a hug. She quickly pulled away, then turned back to Arhyen, ready to go.

"My first hug," Hamlet observed. "How odd." With

that, he turned and joined the crowd, rushing forward toward the Queen.

Arhyen protected Liliana with his body as they made their way out of the fray, followed by Ephraim. Once they were free, Ephraim grabbed Arhyen's arms and stopped him from running further.

He turned back to meet Ephraim's gaze.

"I intend to see this through," Ephraim explained. "This is my city. My home. I need to stay and set things right."

"Then we'll stay with you," Liliana blurted.

Ephraim shook his head. "I know this city has done no favors for either of you. It cannot be your destiny to restore it. Now *go*." He turned back to the crowd.

"But you might be killed!" Liliana gasped, grabbing hold of his sleeve.

Ephraim looked back over his shoulder at her and smirked. "My dear, it will take much more than *this*," he gestured toward the chaos, "to kill the great Ephraim Godwin."

Arhyen shook his head ruefully. That *would* be Ephraim's parting line. "We'll stop at my uncle's farm in the South for a few days while we search for a ship to grant us passage. Try to send word if you can."

Ephraim nodded, then clasped his hand over Arhyen's shoulder. "You've been a good friend," he paused, "for a thief."

He grinned. "You've been a good friend, for an uptight detective with a major stick up his bum."

Ephraim rolled his eyes, then stepped back, disappearing into the riotous crowd.

Arhyen took Liliana's hand, then smiled down at her. A few guards rushed toward them, attempting to bar their escape.

"Time to go, my dear," he announced.

She hesitated, glancing back over her shoulder, but finally nodded.

The guards charged them, but expecting to enter into combat with humans, were taken off guard as Arhyen darted behind one and crouched, only to have Liliana land a kick on the guard's chest, sending him toppling over Arhyen's back. As the second guard watched his comrade fall, Liliana tripped him, stole his pistol, and hit him in the head with the non-lethal end, knocking him unconscious.

They both ran while they could. Eventually the riot would die down, but London would know the truth. They would be heroes to some, and villains to others.

Either way, it was time to leave London behind.

❧

LILIANA FELT LIKE SHE COULD BARELY BREATHE, AND IT wasn't from the exertion of running. Her heart was torn between excitement and heartbreak. Would she truly never see Ephraim again? And what about Hamlet?

She shook her head and kept running. She'd seen Hamlet on their way to the palace, darting across rooftops and behind buildings. He'd been running with them the entire way, staying just out of sight. It was how she'd known they would be alright approaching the palace, even with all of the guards waiting on the perimeter. She knew Hamlet would not let them go down without a fight.

Though her heart was breaking to leave Ephraim, and even Hamlet, behind, Arhyen's hand grasping hers as they ran was the only thing that felt truly real to her in that moment.

"We're being chased," Arhyen hissed, drawing her out of her thoughts.

Suddenly he darted to the right, pulling her along with him. They ran full speed down an alleyway, their footfalls echoing back and forth between the brick buildings on either side of them. At the end of the alley, they turned left to run down another.

"By whom?" she gasped as he tugged her into another sharp turn.

A moment later, her question was answered as she spotted a man in a Queen's Guard uniform running down a parallel street. He disappeared from sight as they passed the intersection, then reappeared at the next.

"He's running too fast to be human!" she rasped.

"Mhmm," Arhyen responded, not missing a step. "It would stand to reason the Queen would make use of her own technology. With automatons in the Queen's Guard, they would be nearly unstoppable."

She didn't like the sound of that, but seeing no other choice, she continued running at Arhyen's side. They would face the guards when the time came. Now that they had come this far, nothing would stop her from leaving the city to start her new life. Not the guards, not Hamlet, not even the Queen herself.

❧

THE CITY GATE WAS IN SIGHT, BUT SO WERE THE guards. Arhyen had no doubt by this point that they were either full automatons, or altered humans, like him. They'd kept pace with them too easily, and now they were flanking them, preparing to cut off their escape. He should have known the Queen would have a trick up her sleeve to prevent them from leaving the city.

He and Liliana both halted as seven guards moved to block their way. The guards turned on their heels, then simultaneously aimed rifles at Arhyen's chest.

"What do we do?" Liliana whispered.

He eyed each of the guards, calculating their odds of escaping without getting shot. Liliana would likely survive a few wounds, but he was not sure of his own durability. The only remaining vial of medicine was in his safe back at the apartment. They'd have nothing to help heal their wounds, and would be hard pressed to make the long journey to his uncle's farm on foot.

"I'll distract them," he whispered. "You run."

"No," she argued. "I will not leave you. We will fight our way through."

"That won't be necessary," a voice explained from behind them.

Arhyen didn't have to turn to see who it was. He would recognize that voice anywhere. Hamlet stepped around them, then placed himself in front of Arhyen, blocking him from the armed guards' view.

He spread his arms as he faced those blocking the gates. "I assume you would all rather capture a terrorist, than a lowly thief?"

The rifles didn't move.

"Whose orders are they awaiting?" Liliana whispered, leaning close to Arhyen's shoulder.

The surrounding area was so silent, Arhyen thought he could hear a pin drop. Instead, he heard footsteps coming from somewhere near the guarded gate. To his astonishment, out walked Wakefield to stand amongst the rifle-wielding men.

"They await *my* orders," Wakefield answered, though Liliana had barely whispered her question.

Arhyen shook his head. This didn't make sense.

They'd left Wakefield back near the palace amongst the mob. There was no way he could have gotten here so quickly, no way he could have overheard Liliana's question, unless . . . "

"You're an automaton," Arhyen concluded.

Wakefield inclined his head. "I'm surprised it took you this long to figure it out. Codename Hamlet knew from the start."

Liliana leaned to peer around Hamlet toward Wakefield. "You two were working together?" she questioned, obviously confused.

Wakefield snorted and took a few steps forward. "Hardly. Hamlet is a much older . . . unit than I. His inconsistencies led to my creation. Unlike him, I would never harm innocents. He cornered me last night after he escaped from the palace. I knew I could not best him physically on my own. He was trained to be a killing machine, impervious to pain. The best I could do was make a deal. He wanted me to claim he'd been destroyed, and in return, he would harm no more innocents."

Arhyen watched Hamlet's back as he nodded, verifying everything Wakefield had said. Without turning around, he explained, "I knew the Queen would remain in hiding until she thought I had been destroyed. I only had to follow you, Mr. Croft, to figure out your plan, and as you know, I have many spies. I knew you would never go along with what the Queen requested. And so, I waited. All I ever wanted was for the public to know the truth, to understand the cruelty of those who created me. Now, they know."

"And now," Wakefield picked up, "I will carry out my final duty. You, Codename Hamlet, must be eliminated for your crimes against your queen."

"But you betrayed her too!" Liliana blurted, pulling

away from Arhyen and stepping forward. "You verified that we were telling the truth. Doesn't this mean you're on our side?"

"There are no sides," Wakefield replied almost sadly. "Only right and wrong, and my duty is to the Queen. I will be punished for my betrayal, just as Hamlet must be punished for his."

"Allow Mr. Croft and Ms. Breckinridge to escape," Hamlet offered calmly. "Allow them to pass unharmed, and I swear to you, I will not run. I will fight, but I will not run. We can both go down in flames together."

Wakefield visibly stiffened, glancing back at his armed men, armed *automatons*, then back to Hamlet. "You would sacrifice yourself for them? Why?"

Hamlet chuckled. "Just as you must carry out your final duty, so must I carry out mine. He loves her," he stated, gesturing back toward Arhyen. "A man who started out human, is able to see past everything she is. He would sacrifice his own life for her, an automaton. Do you not think that is something worth saving?"

Everyone was silent for what seemed like minutes, but was merely seconds. Arhyen could hardly believe his ears. He knew Hamlet would do what it took to save Liliana, but to hear he wanted to save him too . . .

Suddenly, Wakefield burst out in laughter. He doubled over, slapping his knee. His automaton soldiers stared at him in seeming disbelief.

Eventually he straightened, affixed his gaze to Hamlet, and nodded. "Yes, I suppose that is something worth saving." He peered past Hamlet to Arhyen. "You and the young lady may pass, Mr. Croft. I thank you for your cooperation. My men will all attest to the fact that you were killed. No one will follow you."

He could hardly believe his ears. He turned to Liliana.

"Are you ready?"

She met his gaze, then turned to Hamlet, who was finally looking back at them. "I can't just let you sacrifice yourself," she muttered. "It isn't right."

Turning his back on Wakefield, Hamlet stepped toward her, then reached a gloved hand out to cradle her face. "The world isn't right," he whispered. "We must all play the hands we've been given. You've been dealt a chance that few of us will ever know. It is not right, nor wrong, it is simply life. The only promise I ask of you, is that you live it."

Liliana dove forward and hugged him, weeping against his chest. Arhyen couldn't help but consider that this was only the second hug Hamlet had ever received. He wasn't sure why that should matter, but it did.

Liliana slowly pulled away, revealing her tear-streaked face. "I'll do what you think is right," she replied to Hamlet, "but it won't stop me from hoping that you'll survive this to find your own happiness, even after all you have done."

He chuckled. "While I do not believe I deserve happiness after the crimes I've committed, I do believe you've just given me the motivation to fight with all I'm worth. Now go, before Captain Wakefield changes his mind."

Liliana nodded, then turned back to Arhyen, extending her hand. He took her small hand in his, nodding his thanks to Hamlet. He may have wished for the automaton's death one hundred times over, and after all that he'd done, he still did, but he would not deny that he now owed Hamlet his life, if he didn't already.

They both turned back toward Wakefield and his men, who'd parted to make an open path through the gates. Together they hurried forward, not looking back.

EPILOGUE

It took them three days to reach Arhyen's uncle's farm, and they'd remained there for five days since. Just as Wakefield had assured, no one followed them. Unfortunately, they still had worries. What had become of Ephriam? And what of Wakefield and Hamlet? Arhyen found he was even concerned for his mother. Was he leaving her behind in a city on the brink of a civil war?

He gazed out at the green fields from his seat on his uncle's porch. Though he hadn't seen the man in over a year, he'd graciously taken Liliana and Arhyen in until they could find passage on a ship.

As if summoned by his thoughts of her, Liliana emerged from the house, carrying two cups of tea. She handed one to him, then sat down on the bench and snuggled up by his side.

She had shared in his concerns about everyone, most of all Ephraim. They both knew the man was more than resourceful and could take care of himself, but it hurt to leave him behind.

Arhyen turned his gaze toward the noonday sun to find his uncle's lanky form silhouetted in the light.

"You have a letter," his uncle explained upon reaching them. His lined face impassive, he dipped his hand into the front pocket of his well-worn work shirt and pulled out an envelope. He offered it to Arhyen, then took a long drag on his pipe.

"Thank you, uncle," he replied, taking the letter in hand.

His uncle shrugged, then meandered off, not concerned with the letter's contents. He was only concerned with his land, his crops, and the tiny microcosm of his own life, something Arhyen envied. He never understood why his mother hadn't chosen to remain with her brother, outside of the city where things might be tough, but were at least peaceful.

Liliana watched him expectantly as he set his teacup on the bench and opened the envelope.

After unfolding the enclosed parchment, he scanned the first few lines, then jumped to the bottom. He smiled and lifted his gaze to Liliana. "It's from Ephraim," he explained.

She squealed in delight as he offered her the letter. Grasping it firmly in her small hands, she began to read out loud:

"To whom it may concern,

I am alive and well, thanks for asking. After the riot at the palace, we were in for quite an interesting time. The Queen of England has been deposed, unable to remain in office after news of her crimes reached parliament. Members of the Queen's Guard brought word that the man and woman who'd started the riot were killed, though no bodies were found. I took this to be a mistruth, as I know my friends would not go down so easily. The Captain of the Queen's Guard, a man by the name of Wakefield, is also missing, which is likely for the best, as his ranks will soon undergo massive reform.

Amongst all of these changes, the great city of London has begun to rebuild. The Watch is currently recruiting new officers, with the most capable of new Captains at their head (I'm referring to myself). Though I've never approved of thieves, and can only detest them more in my role as Captain of the Watch, I must admit, I am honored to have called the two of you friends. I can only hope you will write to me once you reach Egypt. I will eagerly await accounts of your adventures, and perhaps will even keep you abreast of mine. Perhaps we'll even meet again some day, in a new London that I'm sure you would both like to see.

Sincerely,

Ephraim Godwin.

P.S. Codename Hamlet seems to have disappeared along with Captain Wakefield and all of the automatons who took part in Hamlet's schemes. If you hear from Hamlet, could you perhaps prompt him to turn himself in? He still has many crimes for which he must answer."

ARHYEN CHUCKLED AS LILIANA FINISHED READING THE letter.

She met his gaze with a grin.

He stood and offered her a hand, pulling her up into

his arms. "Are you ready to go look for that ship now?" he questioned.

She laughed as he extended his arm and twirled her like a dancer, the letter fluttering in her free hand. "Of course! Let's pick up plenty of parchment on the way. I want to give Ephraim an account of our entire voyage!"

Grinning, he pulled her back toward him, then sealed the deal with a kiss. As he pulled away, he whispered, "I love you Liliana Breckinridge, as much as any man is capable."

She giggled. "And I you, Arhyen Croft, as much as any automaton is capable." She grinned mischievously. "Which only means," she added, "that I love you *far* more than is humanly possible."

THE NEXT MORNING, THEY BEGAN THEIR SEARCH FOR A ship. It would take time to find passage, but Arhyen had no doubt they would make it work. They did not know when they would return, nor where life would take them in the end. All they knew, was that as long as they had life in them, they would live it.

CURSING TO HIMSELF, EPHRAIM SHIFTED HIS GRIP ON the chisel, aiming it at the lock that sealed Arhyen's safe. Now that his friend had left the city, he couldn't risk the apartment being cleared out with certain valuables still inside.

Inhaling deeply, he slammed his mallet down onto the chisel, breaking the lock. Setting his tools aside, he lifted the metal hatch and peered down at the safe's contents. The first object he noticed was a vibrant green stone, a creation of the late Victor Ashdown. He carefully lifted out the stone along with the final vial of blue medicine, then the accompanying journal containing the formulae for synthetic emotions.

Finally, he lifted out the currency stored in the bottom of the safe, wondering if it was too late to send it along to Arhyen's uncle's farm. Perhaps he could even deliver it himself. He'd been there once to track Arhyen down, and wouldn't mind if Arhyen and Liliana were still there when he arrived.

He leaned back away from the safe and sighed. He could hardly afford the time for a vacation. London was in ruins. A new civil order was in the works.

He looked down at the electricity stone still in his hand, wondering what other scientific discoveries would soon come to light. He smiled. There were many mysteries still to be solved, and the great Ephraim Godwin was most certainly the man for the job.

The story continues from Ephraim's point of view in the Flowers of Antimony Series, coming soon.

NOTE FROM THE AUTHOR

I hope you enjoyed this installment in the Thief's Apprentice Series. Please remember to leave an honest review! For News and updates, please sign up for my mailing list by visiting:

http://saracroethle.com

Made in the USA
Middletown, DE
21 November 2017